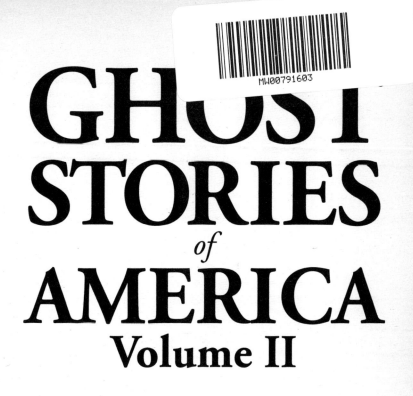

GHOST STORIES
of
AMERICA
Volume II

A.S. Mott

GHOST HOUSE

Ghost House Books

© 2003 by Ghost House Books
First printed in 2003 10 9 8 7 6 5 4 3 2 1
Printed in Canada

The Publisher: Ghost House Books
Distributed by Lone Pine Publishing
10145 – 81 Avenue
Edmonton, AB T6E 1W9
Canada
Website: http://www.ghostbooks.net

National Library of Canada Cataloguing in Publication Data

Asfar, Dan, 1973–
 Ghost stories of America / Dan Asfar & Edrick Thay.

Vol. 2 written by Allan Mott.
 ISBN 1–894877–11–X (v. 1)—ISBN 1–894877–31–4 (v. 2)

 1. Ghosts—United States. 2. Legends—United States. I. Thay, Edrick, 1977– II. Mott, Allan, 1975– III. Title.

GR105.5.A83 2002   398.2'0973'05   C2002–910730–X

Editorial Director: Nancy Foulds
Project Editor: Christopher Wangler
Illustrations Coordinator: Carol Woo
Production Coordinator: Gene Longson
Cover Design: Gerry Dotto
Layout & Production: Jeff Fedorkiw
Photo Credits: Every effort has been made to credit photographers. Any errors or omissions should be directed to the publisher for changes in future editions. The images in this book are reproduced with the kind permission of the following sources: Museum of History and Industry, Seattle (p. 22); Lynett McKell (p. 28); The Stratford Historical Society (p. 33); Bullock Hotel (p. 66, 69); Chico Hot Springs Resort (p. 73, 78); Myrtles Plantation (p. 120, 123); Jeff Black/Molly Brown House Museum (p. 144); Craig Becker/Portland Museum of Art (p. 181); Eric Kvalsvik/White House Historical Association (p. 189); National Archives, Still Pictures Branch (p. 209); Jeff Holbrook (p. 220); Mark Ledford (p. 235, 238); Ernie Dean/Arkansas History Commission (p. 245); Library of Congress (p. 12: USF34-042462-D; p. 47: HABS,NM,4-CIM,7-4; p. 54: USZ62-92593; p. 59: B8171-1287; p. 92: USZC4-2343; p. 98: HABS,ORE,3-ORGCI,1-1; p. 102, USZ62-76684; p. 106: USZC4-6668; p. 110: HABS,CAL,43-SANJOS,9-1; p. 114: HABS,AK,18-SKAG,-4; p. 136: USZ62-94037 ; p. 156: HABS,NY,31-NEYO,51-2; p. 170: HABS,DEL,2-PEPIS, 1-5; p. 173: HABS,DEL,2-PEPIS,1-31; p. 176: HABS,DEL,2-PEPIS,1-11; p. 179: HABS,ME,3-PORT,19-2; p. 183: USZ62-46804; p. 185: D416-29918; p. 187: USZ62-96041; p. 192: HABS,IOWA,31-DUBU,7-3; p. 200: USZ62-40566; p. 206: G613-73896; p. 213: HABS,GA,26-SAV,4-1; p. 216: D423-110; p. 222: HAER,GA,24-FOOG.V,1-10; p. 225: HAER, GA,24-FOOG.V,1-16; p. 229: HABS,MISS,1-NATCH.V,3-1; p. 232: HABS,MISS,1-NATCH.V,3-3).

The stories, folklore and legends in this book are based on the author's collection of sources including individuals whose experiences have led them to believe they have encountered phenomena of some kind or another. They are meant to entertain, and neither the publisher nor the author claims these stories represent fact.

We acknowledge the financial support of the Government of Canada through the Book Publishing Industry Development Program (BPIDP) for our publishing activities.
PC: P5

To Josiah Tatnall,
Who knew how to throw a party

CONTENTS

Chapter 4: Wandering Women

Chapter 5: Haunted History

Chapter 6: Southern Spirits

Acknowledgments

Like a stunned movie star who finds himself on stage with an Oscar, I find that the amount of space I need to thank everyone is woefully inadequate. So, in an effort to get off before the music starts to play, I've made the painful decision to restrict myself to those who have had the greatest impact on this book.

The first person I want to thank is Dan Asfar, who was kind enough to think of me when asked if he knew of any talented writers. Along with Dan, I have to also thank Edrick Thay. Together these vanguards of popular paperback nonfiction wrote the first book in this series, and it was under their influence that I was able to make my way. Their help, however, would have proved useless without the raw material provided by Ghost House Books' (sadly former) resident researcher, Alana Bevan, who was always the person who did everything that actually seemed like work.

I must also thank my editor, Chris Wangler, whose help proved invaluable, and to whom you, the reader, should be most grateful. As well, I must thank Chris' fellow editor, Shelagh Kubish, who was also a great help. Not being able to imagine this book without the pictures that line its pages and the skillful professionalism of its design, I also have to thank Carol Woo, Jeff Fedorkiw and Gerry Dotto for their important contributions.

And finally, just as the star must acknowledge his director and producer, I must thank Nancy Foulds and Shane Kennedy. Without their support I wouldn't have even been nominated.

Introduction

Something happened as this book began to take shape. It became clear that the stories I decided to cover were taking longer to tell than I had first anticipated. I wasn't surprised. My favorite American ghost stories—many of which cannot be condensed into a page or two—are packed not only with paranormal lore, but also with endlessly interesting background material that reflects more than 250 years of haunted history.

The result is a volume somewhat unlike its predecessor by Dan Asfar and Edrick Thay. Instead of covering all the states in the country, as the first volume did, this collection spans only 38. In place of the concision and broad scope of volume one, I offer more rounded stories that illustrate, in vivid detail, how unique many of America's most famous hauntings are. The stories I selected are the ones that struck me as the most moving, frightening, dumbfounding or just plain interesting. Some are well known and others are obscure, but they are all, in their own ways, fascinating.

The organization of the stories highlights their uniqueness and indicates their place within the ghost story genre. In the chapter entitled Unsolved Mysteries, I look at six incidents for which all explanations, either rational or irrational, feel intrinsically unsatisfactory. The only reasonable response to many of the events in these stories is to scratch your head and try not to hurt yourself thinking about them.

In the second chapter, Haunted Hospitality, I explore the spirits who haunt the places where people go to relax and dine. The ghosts in these stories are as varied in temperament as saints are to sinners. With some of them, the prospect of sharing a room or a meal is as terrifying as watching a puppy chase its own tail, while for others the smartest move you could make when approached by them would be to request another room or ask for your meal to go.

Ghosts of the Frontier, chapter three, is devoted to the ghosts of the Wild West, a time when brave settlers headed out to populate unfamiliar and exciting regions. The men and women in this section all display that wonderful 19th-century combination of innocence, courage and determination—a quality shared by many of the ghosts in the fifth chapter, Haunted History. Dedicated to spirits indelibly connected to the past, this chapter is as educational as it is entertaining.

The fourth chapter, Wandering Women, is dedicated to women whose struggles in life compelled them to return after death. Among them are a melancholy lady who frightens soldiers to avenge her own and her husband's death, a lonely ghost who weeps for the family she left behind and the ghost of a slave who once made a horrible mistake. These female phantoms account for some of the book's most moving characters.

The book's final chapter is about that uniquely American region, the South. Southern Spirits contains my favorite story, "The Eternal Party." I have dedicated this book to the story's protagonist, Josiah Tattnall, whose poise and panache in a time of great personal loss is an excellent reminder of what a gentleman can accomplish when he puts others before himself.

Every chapter in this collection describes a country that is united in its diversity. America is a land that has seen war and welcomed peace; a land that has been touched by dire poverty and by overwhelming wealth; a land where dreams can be realized, shattered and then realized again. If you are reminded of its rich character as you read my stories, then I have achieved my goal as an author.

1
Unsolved Mysteries

Miss Rebel's Classroom
RICHARDTON, NORTH DAKOTA

It was Henry who first noticed it. He hadn't been paying attention to the math problem Miss Rebel was working on and his eyes had wandered to the right-hand corner of the room where the stove sat. Like most rural schools in 1944, the one-room Wild Plum School in Richardton, North Dakota, burned coal for heat during the cooler months. Henry's tired eyes popped open when he saw what was happening. He excitedly jabbed his hand into the air and coughed to get Miss Rebel's attention.

"What is it, Henry?" Miss Rebel didn't even bother to turn away from the blackboard, having become accustomed to Henry's frantic interruptions.

"Something's wrong with the coal bucket!" Henry pointed to it with his finger.

This was a new one.

Along with her seven other students, Miss Rebel turned to look where Henry was pointing. They all gasped when they saw that several pieces of coal were moving in the bucket without any visible aid. The little black lumps began to jump and shake like popcorn kernels in hot oil. The students screamed as the coal shot out of the bucket and flew across the room.

Miss Rebel stared in amazement. This was only her second year of teaching, and she was wholly unprepared for anything like this. As she took in the situation, a chunk of coal hurtled directly towards her face. Purely out of reflex she grabbed it out of the air before it

On an ordinary day in 1944, smoldering coals inexplicably flew from the furnace at a one-room school in Richardton, North Dakota.

smashed into her teeth. The coal trembled and shook as she held it.

The coal scuttle crashed to the floor as she ran to the door. No matter how hard she tried, the petite teacher could not get it open.

"Get down!" she ordered the children.

They all jumped underneath their desks. Miss Rebel dodged the flying coal and dived down under hers. One of the younger students began to cry as she waited for the onslaught to end. Miss Rebel heard something moving above her head. She peeked up and saw that her heavy dictionary was sliding across the desk all by itself. She ducked back down and heard the book thud loudly against the floor.

Down beneath her desk the terrified young teacher smelled smoke in the air.

"Miss Rebel!" she heard Henry shout. "The blinds!"

Miss Rebel jumped up and saw that the blinds on all nine windows were beginning to smolder. A piece of flying coal smashed against the side of her head and drew blood. For the first and only time in her teaching career she uttered a curse word in front of her students.

Before her pupils could marvel over this breach of etiquette, a bright flash of light exploded by the bookcase. The heat of it made everyone wet with perspiration. Now all the students were crying. The bright light subsided, revealing that the bookcase was on fire.

Without thinking, Miss Rebel grabbed her brand new coat from the back of her chair and ran to the bookcase while being pelted by flying black projectiles. She threw her coat over the flames and managed to put the fire out. Bloody and blackened, she leaped towards the telephone that had been installed in the school a week earlier.

"Hazel! It's Pauline!" she shouted to the operator. "I need to talk to Ralph Phillips! Now!"

Ralph Phillips was the head of the local board of education. Within half a minute he was on the phone.

"Get over here!" she yelled at him. "And bring the police and firemen with you!"

When she hung up, she ran back to the safety of her desk. The five minutes she spent underneath it felt like hours, but at the end the coal began to drop to the ground and the blinds stopped smoking.

Whatever had just happened, it seemed to be over. With looks of stunned confusion, she and the children climbed out from under their desks and took in the surreal tableaux that surrounded them. Miss Rebel looked down at the floor and saw that several of the coals were still trembling, although it looked as if all the fight had been drained out of them.

Ten minutes later, Mr. Phillips arrived with the police and volunteer firemen. They were just as shocked by what they saw as the teacher and her students were.

The children were sent home and the school was temporarily closed. Miss Rebel was taken to the local doctor to have her cuts and scrapes attended to.

Mr. Phillips and the local police brought in several experts to examine the small schoolroom. No one found anything that could explain what had happened. Several samples of the coal were sent to the chemistry department at the state college. Other samples of the coal, along with the bucket and the dictionary, were sent to the FBI. Everything proved to be completely normal. Miss Rebel and her students all underwent polygraph tests to determine the veracity of their claims. They all passed.

Eventually the school reopened and everyone reluctantly returned. Miss Rebel and her students were all nervous for the first few weeks, jumping at every accidental noise, but soon the tedium of routine allowed them to relax. The incident was never repeated. To this day, no one has any idea what happened that morning. There were some mutterings afterwards that it had something to do with "molecules and atoms," but for many of those involved the more reasonable explanation was distinctly paranormal. For some unknown reason, a poltergeist of some description had decided that day to have some destructive fun. Whatever the case, Miss Rebel made sure from that point on always to wear an old coat to school.

The Eddy Family
CHITTENDEN, VERMONT

Money is often the skeptic's greatest weapon in the battle to debunk the supernatural. Every time psychics or mediums accept cash to contact the spirit realm, they serve to discredit their profession. No matter how powerful, accurate or unexplainable the results of their work, if it is done for profit then there will always be some doubt about its ingenuousness. That is why, to this day, many have trouble believing the stories told about the Eddy family.

The Eddys were a large rural family from the small town of Chittenden, Vermont. They were either blessed or cursed (depending on your point of view) with a surprisingly powerful connection to the spirit world. Throughout the 19th century, they contacted the dead with the ease it now takes to turn on a television set. But because they accepted money for their efforts, many assumed they were just gifted charlatans. As a result, they were often treated like criminals, and the family suffered horribly because of their abilities. The tortures they endured are evidence enough that if they could have rid themselves of their supernatural powers, then the loss of income would have been more than worth it.

The 13 Eddy children all inherited their powers from their mother, Julia. She, in turn, inherited hers from her Scottish ancestors, including her great-great-great grandmother, who was tried and convicted of witchcraft in Salem, Massachusetts. Luckily for her, though, she was rescued by friends from her prison cell and fled back to Scotland. This type of persecution would become typical for the family throughout the decades.

In 1832, Julia met the hardworking and extremely religious Zephaniah Eddy in the town of Weston, Vermont. Julia had few options in the small rural town, so she married him despite disliking his quick temper and stubbornness. Zephaniah also had doubts about the marriage. He was disturbed by Julia's ability to predict the future and by the strange trances that took hold of her from time to time. Still, he believed that through hard work and prayer these abnormalities would eventually disappear. He was wrong. Over the next 14 years, during which 8 of their 13 children were born (John, Francis, Maranda, William, Sophia, Horatio, Mary and James), Julia's strange abilities only became more powerful. Even worse, in Zephaniah's mind, was that the powers seemed to have been passed down to his children.

Right from the start, it was obvious that they were different. Even as newborns they seemed to be in contact with another world. Their cradles would rock gently by themselves and clouds would form in their rooms, echoing with the sound of distant voices. As the children grew older, they began to see the spirits around them much more clearly. Julia taught them not to fear the dead, but to treat them like they would the living. The children obeyed and made friends with the spirits they came in contact with. They often played games with the spirits of dead children, and looked forward to nightly visits from the ghost of their maternal grandmother, whose death had been predicted by the appearance of a ghostly carriage. Such unorthodox behavior made the Eddys pariahs in Weston, so in 1846 Zephaniah moved the family to nearby Chittenden, hoping that the change in location would put an end to the bizarre phenomena.

It didn't. If anything, the bizarre events became clearer and more frequent. Soon enough, Zephaniah—who had long thought his wife and children were delusional—could no longer deny the apparitions around him. He became convinced that Julia and his children were cursed by the Devil, and that unless the sin was driven out of them they would surely go to Hell. Prayer was the first thing he turned to, but when that failed he began to resort to violence.

Whenever Zephaniah found the children in one of the trances that overtook them, he would immediately pummel them with his fists. Once, when William went into a trance, Zephaniah went so far as to pour boiling water on the boy's back and to place a burning hot ember in his hands. The scars that resulted stayed with William until the day he died. On several occasions, Zephaniah took William and Horatio (the two most often lulled into the trances) out into the forest, where he chained them against trees and tried to starve the Devil out of them. But no matter how horrible the cruelties he inflicted on his children, the ghostly manifestations around them never ceased.

Now certain that his children were possessed by the Devil, Zephaniah sought a way to rid himself of them. In 1857, he found just the opportunity he was looking for. Thanks to the efforts of mediums such as the Fox Sisters and Jonathan Koons, there arose a strong public interest in demonstrations of the supernatural, and Zephaniah was quick to realize that he had a possible fortune on his hands. To this end, he found an agent who was willing to buy four of his children (William, Horatio, Sophia and Mary) in order to exhibit them around the country.

Despite escaping the terror of their father, the four children fared no better on the road. In every town they appeared in they were met by skeptics who used different tortures in an effort to expose any kind of trickery. They were often manacled and forced to hold uncomfortable positions or they were placed in small coffin-like boxes that were then nailed shut. At other times, hot wax was poured over their lips to prevent them from speaking, and it was common for them to be poked with sharp needles while they were in their trances. As much as they suffered during their demonstrations, their time on stage was nothing compared to what they went through off it. In almost every town they were threatened and harassed by those who considered them either the spawn of Satan or connivance tricksters. When they were not literally chased out of town, they were frequently shot at, beaten and stoned. Horatio suffered the worst of it, having once been stabbed and hit in the head by a brick. On one occasion, it was only through luck that William avoided being tarred and feathered.

Zephaniah died five years after he sold his children into this horrible life. Ten years passed after his demise before William, Horatio, Sophia and Mary were able to return home. Although their mother joyously welcomed them, Julia took ill shortly after they returned. The children tended to her needs as she lay on her deathbed. One night, Julia sensed how sad and tired her children were. Wanting them to get some much-needed rest, she insisted that she needed some quiet and told them to leave her room. Knowing she could not take care of herself, they humored her and watched her from where she could not see them. To their delight, though, this soon proved unnecessary when out of the darkness appeared the ghost of their sister Maranda (who had died at the age of 31). Throughout that night and the few that followed, she took care of her dying mother, talking to her and even turning her over with the help of several other spirits.

Not long after Julia's death, her children decided to build an upper section at the back of the family farm house. There they held public séances, charging the visitors—who traveled from all around the country to see them—as much as each one could afford. Despite all the efforts made to discredit them, no one could ever determine how they were able to do what they did. Many left the séances believing that the cost to fake such a spectacle would be ten times more than what the family ever actually earned from one. During these demonstrations, William would be placed in a spirit box, and ghosts of all descriptions would appear fully formed over top of him. Often he would summon up the spirits of lost relatives to the amazed gasps of all present. On several occasions, he even summoned up the spirit of Julia, their beloved mother, who only ever had good things to say about being dead. So popular were these séances that hundreds of people were turned away each year for lack of room. Among those refused admittance was Harry Houdini, who was perhaps the most important supernatural skeptic of the era.

The farm house where all this occurred is now a ski lodge, and very few of the people who stay there have any idea about the history of the building. Even today, the locals view the supernatural with great suspicion; most are loath to advertise the unearthly incidents that briefly made their small town famous. Time took care of the Eddys, and they all eventually joined the spirits they had summoned so easily throughout their lives. Given the degree to which they had suffered at the hands of the living, the reunion seems to have been a blessing. It is tragic to think that a group of people with such a wonderful gift would never really be allowed to enjoy it.

Burnley
SEATTLE, WASHINGTON

It speaks to the innocence of the young that their ghosts are seldom described as vicious or angry. Even those youthful spirits who died under tragic circumstances seem loath to dwell in the misery that so often envelops their adult counterparts. Instead, the ghosts of the young act in much the same way as real children. They like to play games, pull practical jokes and engage in genial mischief. Adult ghosts, on the other hand, are more prone to obsessively recreating the moments of their demise, terrifying the living or making pathetic attempts to gain someone's sympathy.

The ghost who haunts Seattle Central Community College in Seattle, Washington, was, by popular accounts, 18 when he died. Right on the cusp of adulthood, Burnley (as he was dubbed by the school's staff and students, after the name of one of the school's previous incarnations) evidently still possesses the youthful playfulness that quickly fades at the end of childhood. Today his spirit is a playful trickster who, like most 18-year-old boys, focuses his attentions on the opposite sex.

The nondescript, three-story building was built in 1907 on Seattle's Pine Street to house Broadway High School. At the time, nothing distinguished the school from other learning institutions. It would take six years before anything out of the ordinary occurred at the school, but when it did it had a lasting effect.

Thanks to what many believe was an official cover-up, little is actually known about the incident, including the

An early photo of Broadway High School, now part of Seattle Central Community College.

real name of the 18-year-old boy who would eventually be rechristened Burnley. What is known is that the school's gymnasium was located on the building's third floor, and that basketball was the school's premier sport. In 1913, boys were no different than they are now   fiercely competitive and extremely emotional. No one knows exactly what caused the fight that erupted after one game, but those involved were so enraged that they took leave of their senses. One thing led to another, and Burnley was thrown down the narrow back stairs and broke his neck.

Like many ghosts, Burnley took his time before making his presence known. By 1946, the high school had been shut down and had been replaced by the Burnley School of Professional Art. Founded by Edwin and Elise Burnley, the school originally taught illustration and graphic design before expanding to include commercial art. During the 14 years in which the Burnleys owned the school, there were few reports of supernatural activity.

It wasn't until 1960, when Jess Cauthorn bought the school, that tales of strange occurrences began to circulate. Students and staff talked about hearing unexplainable sounds emanating from adjacent or adjoining rooms. They also heard loud footsteps that seemed to follow whoever heard them. Sudden chills would overtake visitors and make them feel uneasy. One night, a janitor heard a loud crash come from a classroom and found, when he checked it out, that four desks had been overturned. Trash had been scattered about and doors, both locked and unlocked, opened and closed without any visible assistance. Assuming at first that these pranks were the work of students, Cauthorn installed an alarm system, hoping to catch them in the act. Immediately after its installation, the alarm sounded almost nightly, but no one was ever caught setting it off.

As the reports became more frequent, an interesting pattern emerged. The majority of the students reporting the incidents were female. Some speculated that Burnley may have returned in the 1960s for two reasons: one was the increase in female students, and the other was the rise in popularity of the miniskirt. When the staff invited several mediums to perform séances at the school, they all identified the spirit as that of the boy who had been killed in 1913. It follows, then, that the spirit of a teenager who had lived at a time when a flash of ankle was considered erotic would be very intrigued by the fashion upheavals of the '60s. It was no coincidence that the prettier students were the ones most likely to report being followed by the phantom footsteps. Burnley, in other words, was girl crazy.

Like many teenage boys, Burnley was prone to playing cruel tricks on girls he seemed especially to like. One incident proved almost fatal, when he nudged a young woman who was standing in front of a third-story window. She almost fell out, but was saved when Burnley's invisible hands grabbed her waist. Other female students reported seeing their working materials (pens, X-acto knives, etc.) roll across flat and level surfaces and fall to the floor.

On the rare occasion when Burnley focused his attention on a male student, it was invariably to pull off a prank. Consider the student who had just finished painting a five-foot-tall posing platform in a classroom on the second floor. He had left the room to get some food from the first-floor dispensers when he heard the loud screech of a heavy object being dragged across a floor. The student ran upstairs and found, to his great astonishment, that the platform he had just finished painting was now on the opposite side of the room. The most bizarre of the male-oriented pranks occurred in 1968 when it was discovered that every male student had torn their left shoelace on the same day.

The Burnley School of Professional Art closed its doors in 1986, and the building became the South Annex of the Seattle Central Community College. Students today are less forthcoming about reporting any strange incidents, but at least one prank has been recorded, and, not surprisingly, the butt of the joke was a woman.

The manager of the school's microcomputer lab was in the storage room taking inventory when a pile of computer disks began to shower down upon her head. She had just checked those disks and knew they were too far away from where she was working to have accidentally fallen on her. She also knew about Burnley and had observed, for herself, his attraction to the women in the building. Because none of his pranks seemed deliberately malicious, she wasn't at all frightened or angry when he tried it again.

"Very funny," she said sarcastically. "Now stop it. I've got a lot of work to do and you're not helping."

Burnley seemed satisfied by her acknowledgment and stopped bothering her. Despite the violence of his death, Burnley's ghost seems much less concerned about the nature of his passing than he is about his close proximity to beautiful women. With a seemingly healthy libido and an impish sense of humor, Burnley seems like an ideal college ghost. He is, in essence, a phantom frat guy, completely free of the neuroses that typically dominate a more mature personality. And if college is, as many claim, the best time of one's life, perhaps it can also be the best time of one's death as well.

Ghostwritten
ST. LOUIS, MISSOURI

As a literary figure, Patience Worth has long been forgotten. Despite her prolific output and the acclaim she received while her books were in print, her name is no longer mentioned in English textbooks. Those few book lovers who do remember her regard her as little more than a historical curiosity. While this could have something to do with the nature of her work, which by today's standards sounds archaic and pretentious, a more likely explanation is that her work has always been overshadowed by the bizarre circumstances under which it was created. For the most striking aspect of Patience's literary output was not the quality of her writing, but that the work existed at all. Without the aid of an uneducated St. Louis housewife named Pearl Curren, Patience would have remained unpublished, since it is very hard for a writer to get the attention of a publisher when she has been dead for 300 years.

Pearl Curren was born Pearl Pollard in a small Texas town in 1883. Her upbringing proved uneventful. Her family consisted of good middle-class people with little imagination and a modest disdain for organized religion and modern education. As such, they had little use for art, history or culture. As a result, Pearl grew up to be somewhat ignorant about the world around her. Like her parents, she seldom read anything and she stopped going to school when she was 14. Save for a brief flirtation with the stage, Pearl had little ambition to be anything other than a housewife. At 24 she married an immigration official named John Curren and moved to St. Louis. For seven years their life there was dull and without incident.

At a time when it was rare for a woman to be employed outside the home, Pearl had to fight against the tedium that made up an average day. Because the Currens were able to afford the services of a maid, she was spared the daily grind of housework, which left her with even more time to kill. Worse, Pearl had no hobbies or interests, apart from attending all the silent films she could see. As her mind began to atrophy from disuse, she grew weary and listless. Little surprise, then, that she would be so receptive to a spirit that had spent hundreds of years searching for a person with whom it could communicate.

July 8, 1913, seemed like just another dull afternoon. Pearl had invited her neighbor over to visit and play with the Ouija board her husband had bought her. Ouija boards (named for a combination of the French and German words for yes) were something of a fad at the time. People would spend hours at the boards trying to contact spirits who would help guide the three-legged pointer over different letters and numbers to answer questions about the future and the afterlife. Pearl and her neighbor had whiled away several afternoons at the board, never getting anything but gibberish. This afternoon would prove much more eventful.

Pearl was a bit bored by the prospect of another attempt at spiritual contact, but she had nothing better to do, so she sat down and placed her hands on the pointer and waited. As always, it began to move, but this time the

With the help of a Ouija board, Pearl Curren contacted the mysterious literary incarnation of Patience Worth.

letters she pointed to actually seemed to spell out a genuine sentence. Her neighbor wrote down the letters, and when Pearl finished they were shocked by what they read.

"Many moons ago I lived. Again I come. My name is Patience Worth. If thou shalt live, so shall I."

Excited, Pearl's neighbor told her to ask the spirit where she was from. Pearl used the pointer to ask the spirit; the answer came back immediately.

"From England across the sea. Could I but hold your ear for the lessons I could teach."

Using the pointer, Patience continued to dictate, saying that she was from the English town of Dorsetshire and that she had been born in either 1649 or 1694 (she pointed to both dates and refused from then on to clarify). She had left England to move to America, where, once she reached Missouri, she had been murdered by Indians. Although she didn't say so at the time, it would soon become evident that Patience had died dreaming of being a writer. Her desire to create was so strong that she spent centuries searching for the right opportunity to come back and fulfill her ambition. Pearl was just what she had been looking for. The housewife's limited intelligence and perpetual ennui presented ideal conditions for the spirit writer to use.

Thrilled by her spiritual connection, Pearl returned eagerly to the Ouija board, day after day. It was then that Patience began to write through Pearl, starting with short poems written in blank verse. Soon enough, the messages from Patience came so fast that it became impossible to write them down. Pearl then realized that she no longer needed the board to communicate with the spirit, as the sentences were now forming clearly in her own mind. She was able to simply dictate the words that the spirit shared with her, speaking them aloud as if they were her own thoughts. Interestingly, though, Pearl was never possessed by Patience in the way that so many spiritual mediums are by their phantom contacts. She was able to share both Patience's and her own thoughts at the same time, and never went into a trance to talk to the ghost, as Patience was always there with her.

As Patience's literary output multiplied, Pearl wondered if the work was publishable. She had little interest in poetry and had no idea if Patience's work was any good. She sent several poems to a publisher and was surprised when they were eagerly accepted, along with a note to send more. Around this time, word had begun to spread about her and Patience's unique spiritual bond, and paranormal enthusiasts from all around the country came to visit them. All were astounded by Patience's ability to immediately answer their questions and by her unique poetic gifts. As a frequent test, skeptics and researchers would ask Patience to create a poem about a specific subject on the spot. She never took longer than three seconds before the verse would begin to fly from Pearl's mouth, coming out so fast that the words had to be recorded in shorthand. When, months later, the same people would ask her to reproduce the poetry, she would do so without changing a single word. Often, when the poems were finished, Pearl would ask either Patience or those assembled the meaning of words she had recited but not understood.

Not content to work only as a poet, Patience used Pearl to help create several novels. The first, a massive epic entitled *The Sorry Tale*, was an extremely accurate account of the time of Christ, full of specific details that the uneducated Pearl would have had no way of knowing. The book received glowing reviews, and some critics called it the best work about the period since the gospels. Although the team's situation was well publicized—thanks in part to Casper Yost's book *Patience Worth: A Psychic Mystery*—many reviewers had no idea they were reviewing the work of a ghost.

To those who remained skeptical of Patience's existence, the most perplexing of her novels was *Telka: A Medieval Idyll*. Completed in just 35 hours, the 70,000-word book was written partly in iambic pentameter without the use of a single word that did not exist before 1700. Those who had met Pearl recognized that the work was far beyond her mental abilities. This theory was further supported when, inspired by Patience's creativity, Pearl decided to do some writing on her own. Eventually two of her stories appeared in the *Saturday Evening Post*, but the difference in quality between them and Patience's work was obvious—especially to Patience, who gently mocked Pearl's ambitions.

Although Patience would have remained a nameless spirit without Pearl, the supremely self-confident ghost often treated her host with a patronizing hauteur. She would chide her medium whenever Pearl questioned the meaning of a word or an entire poem, telling her impatiently that it didn't matter if she understood it as long as she wrote it down correctly. Around 1922, the relationship between the two became strained when Pearl became pregnant and had less time to spend working on Patience's writing. Consequently, Patience's output greatly decreased, and over the next 15 years she was forgotten by a literary world that had been so quick to embrace her. In 1937, Pearl died and Patience's writing career ended permanently.

Despite all the evidence to the contrary, some still dispute that this phantom writer ever existed. They believe that she was an out-and-out fraud perpetuated by a woman far more clever than she appeared. Others are convinced that Patience was an unconscious figment of Pearl's imagination that allowed her to explore talents she had previously neglected. While both of these explanations are compelling, they are, in their own ways, every bit as unsatisfactory as the idea that Patience actually existed.

In any event, it is a pity that her work has been so easily forgotten. She had spent centuries searching for the right person to be her creative conduit, only to see her work dismissed after a few decades. Perhaps, then, the story of Patience Worth and Pearl Curren is a cautionary tale about the fickleness of fame and how writers, no matter who (or what) they are, are only as good as their last story.

Phelps Mansion
STRATFORD, CONNECTICUT

Dr. Eliakim Phelps was growing frustrated with his experiments in spiritualism. The Presbyterian minister, who had long harbored an interest in the occult, had taken part in several séances to contact the dead. But for all his trouble he had yet to make any meaningful contact—or so he thought. He would soon discover that some spirits make it their business to stay hidden until the best opportunity presents itself.

Very little is known about Goody Bassett. She was hanged as a witch almost 200 years before the Phelpses moved into their large Connecticut mansion. Like many stories of accused witches, hers is a tale of intolerance and injustice. Why she chose to torment the Phelpses and why she focused her attention on just two of their four children is unclear. Some have theorized that the children, Harry and Anna, both possessed auras attractive to the dead, while their siblings did not. Whatever the case, Goody did her best to terrorize them, and after eight long months the Phelpses fled a house that was no longer a home.

Goody, a malicious poltergeist, forced the former owners of Phelps Mansion to move away.

Goody's first appearance at the house made quite an impression. The Phelpses were returning home from church when they found that their front door was open and draped with dark black cloth. Unaccustomed to burglars who decorated the houses they broke into, the family entered the house and walked into their parlor. Mrs. Phelps was the first to scream, but the children quickly followed. On top of a table they all saw the ghost of a shrouded corpse. Mrs. Phelps and the children ran out of the house, but Dr. Phelps, who had anticipated something like this for some time, stayed and observed the apparition until it faded into thin air.

The incident was Goody's first hint that she wanted the Phelpses to leave. The second hint appeared just a few minutes later when the family, assured by Dr. Phelps that everything was now safe, went upstairs. What they found was, in its own way, even more disturbing than the ghost on the table. On each of their beds they found their clothes laid out, arranged to appear as if they were dead bodies, with the arms folded across their chests. The meaning could not be any clearer.

Determined not to be forced out of his home, Dr. Phelps calmed the fears of his family and convinced them that the ghost was only capable of empty gestures. They tried to take this advice to heart, but found it hard when a few days later Harry found a collection of life-sized dolls made from stuffed clothing, lined in a row in the main room. The dolls were designed to look as though they were praying. This display was taken to be a suggestion that the spirit had only disdain for the family's religious beliefs. As the weeks passed, more and more of these dolls were found throughout the house. Then, without warning, things got much worse.

Household objects began to move by themselves, and loud bangs and crashes could be heard echoing in the house at all hours of the day. Afraid that no one would believe what was happening, Dr. Phelps invited another clergyman to stay at the house and serve as a witness. Dr. Phelps' guest stayed for three weeks, and in that time saw furniture levitate and a large ornate candlestick holder leap from the mantel and slam repeatedly against the floor until it shattered. An alert witness, he observed that the supernatural events only occurred when either Harry or Anna was in the room. No one could explain why the spirit was so attracted to them and not the others.

Soon news spread throughout the state about the inexplicable occurrences at Phelps Mansion. Reporters, scientists and psychics all made it their business to observe what was happening. They were not disappointed. Many heard the loud noises and saw heavy objects float through the air under their own power. Some saw objects tumble and fly across a room, crashing through windows. These experts helped identify the ghost, but her motivations and intentions remained a mystery. Based on her behavior, she was categorized as a poltergeist—a malevolent breed of ghost who takes a sadistic delight in creating chaos and disorder. Unlike other ghosts, who tend to act out scenarios related to their former lives, poltergeists often operate without motive or reason. They do it for kicks.

For a while, Dr. Phelps actually enjoyed the attention he and his house were receiving. The family grew accustomed to Goody's rampages, and Harry and Anna sometimes exploited her presence by blaming her for accidents they caused. The Phelpses were content to share the house with their poltergeist until one event made them seriously question the wisdom of staying.

The doctor and his wife were asleep when a thumping sound erupted from across the hall. Long accustomed to such an occurrence, they didn't even bother opening their eyes.

"Mama!"

The sound of Anna's screams caused the parents both to bolt upright. Henry's screams soon followed.

"Papa!"

The parents leaped from their bed and ran to the children's bedroom. They watched in shock as Harry and Anna thrashed with an unseen force in their beds. Their bodies were being slammed up and down and tears were streaming down their cheeks. The doctor ran to Harry and his wife ran to Anna. While trying to lift the children away from their beds, they were both flung aside by what felt like a powerful wind.

"Damn you!" Dr. Phelps screamed helplessly at the ghost.

Joined now by their two other children, the four made another attempt to rescue Harry and Anna. Again another blast of air rocketed them off their feet.

Harry and Anna screamed for help as Goody began to shake them even harder.

Tears were in Dr. Phelps' eyes as he tried to figure out what to do. He grabbed his wife's hand and began to pray. All of a sudden an idea popped into his brain. It was so simple he was ashamed he had never thought of it before.

"You win, Goody," he announced. "The house is yours. I give it to you. We will be out within the week."

A blast of wind blew past him, and Harry and Anna stopped shaking. The doctor and his wife ran to them and saw that they were terrified but uninjured. The next day Dr. Phelps set about keeping his promise, ordering his family to pack up their belongings. By the end of the week they were out of the house, never to return.

Goody, it would appear, got what she wanted. She did not follow the Phelpses to their new home; in fact, she put an end to her games at the mansion. Why she focused on Harry and Anna and why she wanted the house to herself remain unknown. This is in keeping with the behavior of many poltergeists, who leave motives to more typical kinds of ghosts. Perhaps Harry and Anna truly did possess elusive qualities that made them attractive to a destructive spirit like Goody, or maybe she merely found pleasure in targeting the innocent. Whatever the case, she is gone now—hopefully never to return.

A Vision of Yesterday
LINCOLN, NEBRASKA

Founded in 1887 by a group of philanthropically minded
Methodists, Wesleyan University in Lincoln, Nebraska,
has grown into one of the top liberal arts colleges in the
central west. Like many learning institutions, it experienced many ups and downs during the 20th century. In its
early years, it teetered on the edge of bankruptcy and
often suffered dips in enrollment during periods of
American unrest, such as the stock market crash of 1929
and the two world wars. Eventually, though, the school
was able to resolve its financial woes.

Today, the university bears little resemblance to the
gothic brick structure that served as its first building
(which, during its first year of operation, did not have
stairs. Both staff and students were required to climb lad-
ders to get to classes on the upper levels). At the time it
was built, the school was surrounded by empty land, but
as Lincoln grew it came to be surrounded by a variety of
different buildings, which also changed greatly with the
times. One of the first buildings to be added to the school
was the C.C. White Memorial Building, which was built
between 1903 and 1907. It was in this building that the
music department held all its classes; it was also where a
young secretary briefly found herself transported to
another time.

In 1963, Coleen Buterbaugh was Dean Sam Dahl's secretary. Fairly new to the job, she found herself in the C.C.
White Building on a mission to track down a visiting

professor from Scotland named Dr. Tom McCourt, who had been given use of several of the music department's rooms. Classes had just ended, and it was an effort for her to walk against the tide of departing students to get to the room where Dr. McCourt was most likely to be. By the time she got to the room, her cheeks were flushed and her breathing was heavy. She looked as though she had just run an obstacle course. With a sense of accomplished relief she knocked on the door. To her impatient disappointment, her knocks were not greeted with any verbal acknowledgment. She tried again.

"Dr. McCourt?" she spoke up as she knocked.

Again she was met with silence.

Knowing that some professors easily become oblivious to the world around them, Coleen opened the door and peeked inside. The room was dark, but she could see the shadowy figure of a person in a corner by the bookshelf. Assuming it was Dr. McCourt, she walked into the room. It was warmer than usual inside and bore the indelicate smell of age and mildew.

"Dr. McCourt?" she repeated, trying to get the figure's attention. The person at the bookshelf did not respond.

"It's a little dark in here," Coleen remarked. "Do you mind if I turn the lights on?"

The figure did not respond, but Coleen assumed silence indicated consent, so she flicked on the lights.

It was then that she saw that the shadowy figure was not Dr. McCourt at all. The figure was a tall, thin woman in her mid- to late thirties. Her hair was dark and bushy in an antiquated way, similar to that worn by women in old sepia-toned photographs. She wore a long-sleeved white blouse, a long skirt with coarse stockings and a pair of heavy oxford shoes. Too old to be a student, the woman did not strike Coleen as a faculty member.

"Excuse me," Coleen tried again, "but have you seen Dr. McCourt?"

The woman remained silent and continued to search for some papers on the top shelf of the bookcase. Briefly taken aback by the woman's rudeness, Coleen was then further stunned by what she saw outside the room's window—or, rather, by what she *didn't* see.

Instead of the expected leafless autumn trees and sturdy campus buildings, Coleen saw only a bright sunny sky and an expanse of empty land that faded towards the horizon.

"What the—" Coleen stuttered.

As she stared out the window, the woman at the bookcase did something extraordinary. In fact, she did the only thing that could possibly shock Coleen more than the improbable view from the window. She faded from view. Not instantly, as if she had been switched off, but as if she had been connected to a dimmer switch that was slowly being turned down by some mysterious force.

Already a little lightheaded from before, Coleen came dangerously close to losing consciousness. Somehow, though, she managed to remain alert. Although the woman had faded from sight, she had not left the room.

"Hello?" Coleen's voice sounded more curious than frightened. "Are you still here?"

The smell in the room, which had seemed muted and distant when she first entered, was now much more palpable. It brought tears to Coleen's eyes and made her cough. Her stomach began to tremble nauseously and her curiosity was quickly replaced by a sense of dread. Seconds away from vomiting, she threw open the door and ran out of the room. The door slammed behind her and Coleen was immediately greeted by a blast of cool air that eased her physical discomfort.

The hall was now empty, save for the sound of marimba music from a nearby classroom. Coleen stood quietly for a minute to collect her thoughts and ease her stomach before she walked into the classroom next to the one that she had just been in. This room was cool and smelled only of chalk dust. Coleen ran to the window and was relieved to see the trees and buildings she had grown accustomed to seeing. She left the room and walked back to Dean Dahl's office in a daze.

When she got there, the dean asked her if she found Dr. McCourt. Not caring that he might think her crazy, Coleen told him about what had just happened to her. It happened that Dean Dahl was a believer in supernatural phenomena, and with his help Coleen was able to figure out what had happened to her.

Together they assumed the phantom Coleen encountered had most likely been a faculty member sometime during the university's history. They searched backwards through yearbooks, starting from 1950, in the hopes that a picture of the woman would surface. They went through 14 books before they found what they were looking for. While flipping through the pages of the 1936 yearbook, Coleen shouted suddenly and pointed to a picture of a woman identified as Clara Urania Mills.

"That's her!"

Clara Mills, it turned out, had been a music teacher at the university from 1912 to 1936. The room in which Coleen had seen the ghost had been Clara's office. The picture Coleen found was of an older Clara than the specter she had encountered. She and Dean Dahl did some more research and discovered that Clara was 60 when she died in 1940. They also discovered that Clara died on October 3, meaning that her supernatural appearance coincided exactly with the 23rd anniversary of her death. With this information they were able to determine that the spirit Coleen saw was from around 1914 to 1918. Using those dates as a reference point, the pair searched through some period photographs and found that they corresponded exactly with what Coleen saw when she looked out the window. It appeared, based on this evidence, that Coleen had not just seen a ghost, but she had actually been transported, however briefly, to another time.

While the questions of who, what, where and when in this case have all been satisfactorily explained, there still remains the question of why. The most obvious clue is the confluence of dates. Coleen saw Clara on the same date on which Clara had died 23 years previously, but as intriguing as that is, it does little to offer any real explanation. It also fails to account for why Coleen was transported to that earlier part of Clara's life. If the date of Clara's death was so important, why didn't Coleen see an older woman in her 60s? And what reason would Clara have for appearing anyway?

While some believe that these questions can be traced back to Coleen's brief time warp (where there would have to be no reason for Clara's appearing, beyond the fact that she was there when Coleen flashed back), such an explanation fails to take Clara's ghostly fade into account. All in all, the pieces to this puzzle have thus far proven too complicated to put together. There is a good chance that they will remain nothing more than the fascinating conundrums that they are.

2
Haunted Hospitality

The St. James Hotel
CIMARRON, NEW MEXICO

It was John Wilkes Booth who first persuaded Henry Lambert to go west to make his fortune. Born in France, Henry had made his name as the personal chef of President Lincoln. When the president was assassinated, the young man put aside his impressive culinary skills and became a gold prospector.

It didn't take long for him to figure out that the rustic life of a miner was not for him. He returned to cooking and soon started to make big money off men who were able to profit from prospecting. His skills brought him to the attention of Lucien Maxwell, one of New Mexico's wealthiest and most powerful men, who offered Henry a job as his personal chef. This meant Henry would have to move to Maxwell's home in Cimarron. Sensing an opportunity, Henry took the job and made the New Mexico town his home.

Not content to spend the rest of his life cooking for just one man, Henry spent his spare time planning and building what would become Lambert's Saloon and Billiard Hall. This proved to be the smartest move of Henry's life. Cimarron was located on the final leg of the famous Santa Fe Trail and received an inexhaustible supply of travelers looking for a place to have a good time and unwind. Henry's saloon became so successful that he was able to stop working for Mr. Maxwell and focus entirely on his business. Eight years later, the building was renovated to include 30 additional hotel rooms. Henry named this new enterprise the St. James. Little did he know that someday the hotel would attract as many supernatural enthusiasts as road-weary travelers.

It is considered a matter of historical record that at least 26 men died violently within the walls of the St. James. This figure isn't shocking when you look at some of the names on the hotel's guest register. A virtual who's who of Wild West mythology, the register included Jesse James, Billy the Kid, Pat Garrett, Wyatt Earp, Doc Holiday, Bat Masterson and Kit Carson. The famous relationship between Buffalo Bill Cody and Annie Oakley got its start inside the St. James, where the pair also planned and rehearsed what would become their world-famous Wild West Show. The St. James was such a wild place that when Henry's sons replaced the saloon's roof, they noticed that it resembled a piece of Swiss cheese, with almost 400 bullet holes scattered through it. Today it has only 22, which by any standard is still a lot.

The mystery of the St. James, then, is not that it is haunted (as it undoubtedly is), but that it isn't haunted more. One would expect spirits to be hidden in every nook and cranny, but the spirit in room 18 more than compensates for this surprising lack of quantity.

Locked up for many years now, room 18 is home to a ghost so possessive that it is rumored to have taken more than one life. The hotel denies this information, but many believe that the reason room 18 was permanently locked up relates to the mysterious fatalities that occurred inside it.

Death is a fact of hotel life that is seldom advertised. In any big city hotel older than 100 years, the chances are good that almost every room has at one point held a

The ghost of murdered cardsharp Thomas Wright haunts room 18 at the St. James Hotel.

corpse. Moreover, most hotels cannot afford to stop using a room just because a death occurred inside it. If they did, they would soon go out of business. For a hotel to take the drastic step of permanently locking up a room, there has to be the fear that it is not safe for a guest to stay there. The ghost of room 18 has provided good enough reason for this fear, making it clear that anyone who tries to spend the night risks not seeing the daylight ever again.

Thomas Wright, who was destined to become room 18's vengeful wraith, was a gambling man. His game of choice was poker and he was good at it. In the end it was his skill that killed him. Given the sad facts of his death, perhaps Thomas' anger is justified.

The man with whom Thomas was playing that night was none other than the owner of the St. James, Henry Lambert. Henry had gotten far in life by taking chances others wouldn't, and that willingness to take risks led him to make the mistake of his life. Drunk and assured that the straight flush dealt to him was unbeatable, he decided to buy the large pot by making a bet he knew no one would call. He bet the ownership of the St. James and sat back as the other men at the table folded in turn. Finally it was Thomas' turn to fold, but instead he took out his wallet and emptied it on the table.

For a moment Henry felt a pang of worry, but then he looked back down at his cards and once again felt confident that there was no way he could lose. He put down his cards with a smile and began to pull the pile of cash, deeds and chips towards him. He stopped when he saw the smile on his opponent's face. When Thomas put down his cards everyone in the room gasped. He had a royal flush and the pot was his to take. The full impact of what he had done hit Henry immediately. His face turned white and he began to sputter.

"You rotten cheat!" Henry spat out at Thomas. "There's no way you could've had a royal flush! Someone check his sleeves!"

Henry's two large assistants grabbed Thomas, ripped off his coat and rolled up his shirt sleeves. His arms were bare.

"You're banned from my hotel! Banned, I tell you!"

Thomas, accustomed to this kind of behavior from sore losers, merely smiled and shook his head.

"You can't ban me from a hotel I own."

Thomas gathered his winnings, told everyone to have a good evening and made his way to the door. He was leaving when he heard the sound of a gunshot from behind him. The bullet dropped him to his knees. As the blood began to flow from the exit wound in his chest, Henry's men grabbed him and dragged him back to his room—room 18—where he was left to slowly bleed to death. The biggest pot Thomas had ever won had become his biggest bust.

Thomas Wright died knowing that the St. James rightfully belonged to him, which explains both his anger and his unwillingness to leave. Those who have encountered his presence in room 18 have described it as a swirling energy field whose electric ferocity is powerful enough to cause any sane person to flee.

It is a good thing, then, that the hateful power of Thomas' spirit is in some way counteracted by another of the hotel's ghosts. Mary Lambert was Henry Lambert's wife, and it is believed that her spirit keeps Thomas' ghost from leaving his room and terrorizing everyone he comes across.

Mary's presence is announced by the delicate aroma of the perfume she wore as a young lady, a scent that hasn't been manufactured for years. She also provides a feeling of peace and warmth. Her one eccentricity is a fear of drafts. Those who have stayed in her room have reported an impatient tapping sound that can be heard whenever they open the window. The sound stops as soon as the window is closed again.

Experts who have studied the supernatural phenomena of the hotel leave convinced that Thomas and Mary battle nightly over the control of the building, and that Mary has thus far proved the stronger of the two. An employee of the hotel—a young woman named Lisle—made this discovery when she was given the room next to room 18 to sleep in. From the very first night, she found it almost impossible to get a decent night's rest there. Although she never had nightmares or heard loud noises, she awoke in terror time and time again. Suspecting that her ordeal had something to do with her infamous neighbor, Lisle consulted one of the many psychics and ghost hunters who stay at the hotel throughout the year. This woman was a psychic, and after spending some time in Lisle's room she concluded that Thomas attempted to possess Lisle every night, but was always thwarted by Mary. Thomas wanted Lisle's body. With it he would be able to move wherever he desired and attack those who had the temerity to enter the building that was stolen from him.

Thomas is limited in his ability to move around the St. James, but Lisle's room was just within his reach. Each night as Lisle slept, Thomas entered her room and silently crept towards her. As Thomas approached Lisle, Mary was always able to grab him and throw him back into room 18. It was the force of Mary's effort that always caused Lisle to awaken.

Lisle asked the psychic what might happen if she stayed in the room.

"There is the chance," the psychic warned her, "that one day Mary will not be there to save you, or worse, that Thomas will someday have the strength to beat her. Either way you risk losing control of your body and the possible damnation of your soul."

Lisle switched rooms that day, and from that point on she always slept peacefully.

The combative ghosts of the St. James remain for very different reasons. They have turned the hotel into a spiritual battleground in which elemental forces of anger, revenge and violence fight it out with the forces of kindness, forgiveness and peace. It is difficult to imagine either side ever giving up, and it seems clear that they are too evenly matched for one to ever permanently triumph over the other. The people who work and stay at the St. James have to accept that one room is off limits and in another the window should always remain closed.

The Surratt Tavern
CLINTON, MARYLAND

Mary Surratt was remarkably calm the day of her execution. When the authorities arrived to take her to the gallows, she walked proudly and defiantly with her head held high. Her courage deserted her once she reached the noose. Realizing that her death sentence was not going to be stayed by President Andrew Johnson, she began to cry. Tears streamed down her face as she peeked over the gallows' edge to the ground that seemed so far below. It was then that she spoke her last words.

"Don't let me fall."

The executioners didn't. The rope around her neck saved her from hitting the ground. Mary died convinced that she was unjustly convicted of her crimes, and still believes in her own innocence long after her death. To this day she haunts the tavern in Clinton, Maryland, which she once owned and where John Wilkes Booth and David Herold ran to get supplies just hours after Booth shot President Lincoln.

Over 130 years after Mary's death, people still debate whether she was guilty of taking part in the conspiracy to assassinate President Lincoln. Some insist that she was a victim of circumstance—a hapless pawn caught up in the American public's desire for vengeance—while others insist that Mary had indeed helped the men who killed the president, or, at the very least, knew of and supported their traitorous plan.

Mary Jenkins was born in Waterloo, Maryland, in 1823. Her childhood bore no trace of the odd direction in which subsequent events would lead her. At the age of 12, Mary was sent to a Catholic boarding school (although her parents were Protestants). It was there that Mary became deeply religious and converted to Catholicism. An ardent believer in the power of prayer, Mary would frequently get down on her knees and ask God for help during times of trouble.

When she was just 17, Mary married a handsome and successful 28-year-old named John Surratt. They moved to a farm in the District of Columbia and had three children—Isaac, Anna and John, Jr. The family lived on the farm for 12 years, until John purchased 287 acres of land in Maryland's Prince George's County, not far from where Mary had grown up. Soon after, John built a two-story building on the property. He then applied for a food and beverage licence. When his application was approved, he moved his family into the house and opened the Surratt Tavern. In addition to serving food and drink, the tavern provided lodging for travelers and soon became a meeting place for the growing local community. Soon enough, the Surratt Tavern became an official polling office and John was made the local postmaster. Because of this latter development, the town became officially known as Surrattsville.

Life was good for the Surratts. John's position gave him a special status in the community and the tavern's steady business allowed them to live comfortably. They also enjoyed the camaraderie of their customers and could often be heard stating their opinions about the state of the country. Although they were only 13 miles from Washington, DC, John and Mary had little use for the arguments of the Union side in the ever-escalating

Mary Surratt's Washington DC townhouse

battle over states' rights. Not only were they quick
to express sympathy for the Confederates, but it was
rumored that when the Civil War erupted, the Surratt
Tavern became a secret safehouse for Maryland's Confederate underground.

Just over a year after the war started, the Surratts' happiness was shattered when John died suddenly of natural causes. Mary was 39 and had never once considered the possibility of widowhood. Nor was she prepared for the revelation that John had left behind serious debts that would push the family dangerously close to the poorhouse.

Mary's financial woes were made all the more difficult by the realities of the Civil War. Like Mary, those who owed the Surratts money had no way of paying off their debts. She managed to survive by selling off parts of her land. In the end, all that remained of John's original 287 acres was the land on which the tavern stood, which Mary then rented to an ex-policeman named John Lloyd. He continued to use the building as a tavern, while Mary moved to a Washington townhouse she had managed to hold on to. She then padded her income by turning her home into a boardinghouse.

While Mary ran the boardinghouse, she met a man whose family was famous throughout the country for their great talents on stage (and for their ability to consume copious amounts of liquor). John Wilkes Booth was a friend of Mary's youngest son, John Surratt, Jr., who had served as a secret agent for the Confederate army during the war. During his apprenticeship in espionage, he had met the men who would eventually kill the president.

Soon Booth and his fellow conspirators—who at first had planned only to kidnap Lincoln, but were forced to assassinate him—became frequent visitors at Mary's boardinghouse. While people can only speculate how aware Mary was of their activities, it is known that Booth would frequently have long, secret talks with her and that she acted suspiciously during the week that preceded Lincoln's murder.

The most damning of these suspicious acts was a short exchange she had with the man who operated the Surratt Tavern, John Lloyd. About a month and a half before the assassination, Lloyd had been asked by John Surratt and two of the conspirators (David Herold and George Atzerodt) to hide two carbines, some ammunition, 20 feet of rope and a monkey wrench in the tavern. A bit confused by the request, Lloyd agreed, but only because John's mother was still his landlady. He forgot about the strange incident, but was reminded of it when he met Mary as he was returning from a trip to Marlboro. Traveling in the company of Lewis Weichmann, one of her boarders, Mary told Lloyd that the shooting irons that her son and his friends had left at the tavern would soon be needed, but she did not say for what.

Three days later, Mary returned to Surrattsville, again accompanied by Weichmann, and left a package containing a pair of field glasses with Lloyd. She told him that all the hidden objects, along with two bottles of whiskey, should be readied as they would be needed later that day. Lloyd did as he was told.

Around midnight, David Herold ran into the tavern and shouted at the tavern keeper.

"Lloyd, for God's sake, make haste and fetch those things!"

Lloyd got everything together and brought it to Herold, who took only one of the carbines, both bottles of whiskey and the field glasses. Lloyd saw Booth, who he had never met before, sitting outside on his horse. It was then that

Lloyd noticed that Booth's leg was broken. Herold proceeded to tell Lloyd the reason for their visit.

"I am fairly certain that we have assassinated the president."

With that confession, Herold and Booth rode off, leaving Lloyd to stew in the terrible knowledge of his unwitting hand in the conspiracy to murder Lincoln.

Just seven hours after Lincoln was shot, investigators appeared at the door of Mary's Washington boardinghouse. During this first visit, they failed to find any sort of incriminating evidence and left empty-handed. When they were gone, Lewis Weichmann later reported, Mary turned to her daughter Anna and spoke.

"Anna, come what will, I am resigned. I think Mr. Booth was only an instrument in the hands of the Almighty to punish this proud and licentious people."

The investigators returned three days later. This time they managed to find the evidence that had earlier eluded them. The most damning of all was a photograph of Booth that Mary had hidden behind a painting on her mantelpiece. To make matters even worse, Lewis Powell, a known member of the conspiracy, arrived at the house with a pickax while the police were still there. He insisted that he was just a worker hired by Mary to dig a gutter. But when he was brought before her, she claimed to have never seen him before. The police believed neither of them and Mary was immediately arrested. As they prepared to handcuff her, Mary asked to be given a minute to pray. She got on her knees and asked God to save her.

God appeared not to hear her prayers. In exchange for clemency, Lewis Weichmann and John Lloyd implicated

Mary in their confessions. Mary was tried along with seven men by a military commission. Out of these eight defendants, four were sentenced to life in prison and four were sentenced to die. Mary found herself in the wrong group of four. Five out of the nine generals who presided over the commission requested that, owing to her age and sex, her sentence be changed to life imprisonment. President Johnson, the new president, insisted that he never heard this request, although White House staff members would later say that the president had heard it, but refused to grant it because, in his words, she had kept the nest that hatched the egg.

Mary was hanged on July 7, 1865. In an interesting twist, around the same time the Supreme Court ruled that a military court had no jurisdiction over civilians if the civil courts were open. As a result, the trial of Mary's son John was held in civil court, where, with the same evidence and witnesses against him as his mother, he was acquitted. Had the government not been so quick to rush to judgment, there is a good chance that Mary would not have been executed.

Like most buildings of such historical importance, the tavern is now a museum (a fate denied to Mary's Washington boardinghouse, which is now a Chinese restaurant). The building is surrounded by strip malls and fast-food restaurants in a town that changed its name from Surrattsville to Robeystown and then, finally, to Clinton. Owned and operated by the Maryland National Capital Park Commission, the Surratt Tavern has become a place where guides dressed in period garb take people on tours. These guides take care to point out

Mary Surratt, far left, and the other conspirators were hanged on July 7, 1865.

all the tavern's interesting artifacts and describe, in detail, the fate of its doomed owner, making sure not to pass judgment either way.

The guides are not so quick, however, to tell visitors that Mary is still around. They might make mention of her ghost, but it is almost always with a wink or a joke, as if in an effort to distract people from the seriousness of Mary's suffering. This tactic is wise, as tourists are seldom interested in being depressed by the places they visit and there is little that is cheery about Mary's ghost.

Because Mary was entirely convinced of her own innocence, her spirit was quick to return to the tavern where all her troubles began. As long as she refuses to accept her role in the conspiracy, genuine or not, she will not be able to pass on from this world.

Instead, she forever wanders throughout the rooms and hallways of her former tavern. She appears as a vague whisper of a being, floating above the ground with only her face distinct enough to appear human. She does her best to avoid the living, having long ago decided that the people of this world are not even worthy of her contempt. Although Mary tries to remember the good years she spent at the tavern with her husband John—whose untimely death was the catalyst that led to the events that resulted in her own untimely passing—her hatred for the men who tangled her in their webs is too strong to be swayed by pleasant memories.

She is not alone. The voices of her fellow executed conspirators can also be heard in the tavern, although they do not share in her torment. Instead, they excitedly plan and replan an event that has long since passed. They seem unaware that they succeeded in their goal to kill the man who had strengthened the Union and freed the slaves.

It is no wonder that Mary has never appeared when these other spirits can be heard. They are as much to blame for her death as the man who pulled the switch that opened the gallows' trapdoor. Mary cursed them all in the second it took for the rope around her neck to stretch taut and she still curses them today. It never occurs to her that maybe her pain would be less intense if she cursed herself.

The Catfish Plantation
WAXAHACHIE, TEXAS

A familiar ghost story involves a couple with a dream. Together they invest the money they have worked so hard to save and manage to buy the house or business of their dreams, only to see those dreams vanish when confronted by an angry spirit. Perhaps the most famous of these stories involves the Lutzes and the house they bought in Amityville, New York. As told in the best-selling book by Jay Anson and in the hit movie directed by Stuart Rosenberg, the young couple saved their money and with it bought a grand old house. This investment proved unwise when it became apparent that the house was haunted by a murderous wraith. For a while it looked like Tom and Melissa Baker might face the same horrible dilemma. In 1984 they bought an old Victorian-style house in the historic Texas town of Waxahachie. They soon discovered that at least one of the house's spirits was not entirely happy with the new arrangement. Unlike the Lutzes, however, the Bakers' story does not have an unhappy ending.

Tom and Melissa intended to turn the house into a restaurant. As connoisseurs of Cajun cuisine, they had decided to open a Louisiana-style eatery called the Catfish Plantation. They felt that the small house would be perfect for the comfortable establishment they had in mind. But transforming the house into a restaurant would involve a lot of hard work. Because Tom had to finish up some business in Dallas, Melissa started commuting to Waxahachie every day to get the transformation underway.

At the time, she was the only person who had keys to the house and she always worked alone. Consequently, Melissa was shocked and confused when she arrived at the house one morning and found a fresh pot of coffee brewing on the stove. She looked around the house to see who had made the coffee, suspecting that it was probably a homeless person who had found a way in. When she established that the house was empty, Melissa had no explanation for how the coffee (which turned out to be excellent) came to be.

Three weeks later, another strange incident occurred. This time, the gesture was not as polite. Melissa found the large urn she and Tom had bought to make iced tea sitting in the middle of the kitchen floor, filled with all their coffee cups. This second occurrence prompted the couple to do some research into the history of the house.

It soon became clear that one of the previous tenants, a woman named Caroline Mooney, had reason to keep the Bakers away from her old home. Caroline did not believe she was dead and still considered the house hers. At first she had decided to be a good hostess and make some coffee for Melissa, whom she considered an uninvited guest. But as the weeks went on, Caroline grew more frustrated by Melissa's constant comings and goings and became angry when the Bakers began to move their stuff in. The urn full of coffee cups was Caroline's polite way of saying please pack up and leave.

Because of Caroline, a séance was held in the dining room by a psychic named Ruth Jones. Caroline, however, resisted Ruth's charms that night. Instead, the Bakers discovered that they had yet another ghost to contend with. Luckily for them, she proved to be a lot less cranky, although her first appearance at the séance proved that she preferred a dramatic entrance. Ruth, the psychic, had been attempting to contact Caroline's spirit when knocking sounds came from inside the walls and dishes began to rattle in the sink. The lit candle that sat in the middle of the table suddenly exploded in a burst of flame, and the door to the kitchen burst open with a loud bang. From out of the doorway floated the ghost of a young woman dressed in an old wedding gown. She smelled of roses and her presence made the room cold. On her face was a sad, wistful expression. It was later discovered that her name was Elizabeth Anderson and that she had been married in the house. It proved to be an extremely short marriage, as she had been found strangled to death in the house on her wedding day.

Unlike Caroline, who grows more and more angry with all the people coming into her home, Elizabeth takes comfort in the company they bring. Melissa described a typical Elizabeth incident. Alone in the restaurant doing some paperwork, she smelled roses and felt the chill that indicated Elizabeth's presence. Then she felt a cold gentle force grasp her right hand. For 15 minutes she and Elizabeth held hands—a quiet moment of heartfelt companionship.

After the restaurant opened and began to thrive, Caroline made her presence felt much more forcibly than before. She began to throw coffee cups, cans and food whenever her temper flared up. Angered not just by the strangers in her home, but also by the fact that her family had stopped coming to visit her, Caroline is held back only by a natural sense of southern politeness. Otherwise she could easily become a very nasty poltergeist. Although she is unhappy about the present arrangement, the last thing she'll ever be is rude.

Elizabeth, on the other hand, loves the customers and has, on at least one occasion, followed them home. A restaurant patron who had expressed sorrow upon hearing Elizabeth's story awoke in her bed later the same night when she heard the voice of a young woman. She saw Elizabeth hovering beside her bed with an antique figurine in her hands. Elizabeth gave this present to the woman and smiled serenely at her before vanishing. On another occasion, Elizabeth caught the attention of a young family when she wrote the name of their young baby in the condensation on the window they sat next to.

Because of the kindness the Bakers and their employees have shown to Caroline and Elizabeth, another ghost—a farmer named Will who lived in the house during the Depression—has decided to make his presence felt occasionally. A quiet soul, he is most likely to be seen lounging on the front porch, although he sometimes can be sensed hanging out inside, happy to have the company.

The Bakers are very lucky. Despite Caroline's frequent temper tantrums, the ghosts that haunt their dream project have never tried to turn it into a nightmare. In fact, the presence of these unearthly visitors has made the Catfish Plantation a popular tourist spot in Waxahachie. The Bakers' story is a happy reminder that not every supernatural encounter turns out to be an unhappy one.

The Bullock Hotel
DEADWOOD, SOUTH DAKOTA

There are few towns in America with a name as provocative as South Dakota's Deadwood. With the possible exception of Tombstone, Arizona, it is hard to think of a town whose name better represents the grit and determination of the frontier era. The name brazenly suggests that a dandified city slicker should think twice before he rides in because he'll be just as soon rode out.

It comes, then, as something of a disappointment that the origin of Deadwood's name is somewhat pedestrian. Founded in 1876, the gold rush town was named after the dead trees that littered the landscape of the nearby canyon. That same year Deadwood took its place in history when its most famous resident, James Butler Hickok (or Wild Bill, as he was better known), was shot in the back of the head by Jack McCall in the imaginatively named Saloon #10. It was the death of this cowboy legend that led the people of Deadwood to find a sheriff to protect them. To that end, they hired Seth Bullock, an entrepreneur and close friend of Theodore Roosevelt. Bullock brought peace to Deadwood—but that was not his only contribution.

Seth Bullock was born in Sandwich, Ontario, in 1849. The son of an overbearing British major, he felt stifled by his father's strict rules and ran away as soon as he could. Like so many others at the time, he was attracted to the American West and soon became a permanent fixture in its history. Bullock got into politics at a young age,

Pioneer Seth Bullock (left) with friend Theodore Roosevelt

running for various offices before he turned 21. For two years he served as a Republican member of Montana's Territorial Senate, where he made his mark by introducing a resolution to the Federal Congress to set aside Yellowstone as a national park, which it did in 1872. A year later, Bullock was elected sheriff of Montana Territory in Lewis and Clark County, where, along with his duties as a keeper of the peace, he became an auctioneer, firefighter and hardware store owner. Three years later, Bullock left Montana for South Dakota, where in the newly founded city of Deadwood he opened another hardware store. By the end of the year he was Deadwood's sheriff. In the 20 or so years that followed, he successfully cleaned up Deadwood and became a successful business-man, farmer and rancher.

When Bullock's hardware store was destroyed in a large fire, he decided to build a luxury hotel in its place. Finished in 1895, the Victorian-style hotel (which he named The Bullock, after himself) was designed to differ from the flop houses and brothels that were, for a time, the only place a traveler could find a bed in Deadwood. Along with 63 rooms, the hotel contained a full Turkish bath and an ornate reading parlor. From the day it opened, it imme-diately became the place to stay in Deadwood, claiming Bullock's friend Theodore Roosevelt as its most famous guest. In 1905 President Roosevelt appointed Bullock as U.S. Marshall for South Dakota, a position he held for the duration of the Taft administration and for the first year of Woodrow Wilson's presidency.

Having lived a rich and full life, Bullock died in 1919. Soon thereafter, his hotel fell into disrepair and over the passing years became a shadow of what it once was. Sixty-nine years passed before someone decided that the grand hotel should be restored, and when the work was finished, they discovered that Deadwood's famous former sheriff was there to see it happen.

When a woman named Mary Schmit bought the old hotel in 1988, no one suspected that it was haunted. It was only as the restoration process began that reports of unearthly phenomena started to surface. Construction workers noticed that their tools and benches were often not where they left them. Then came the reports of mysterious and unexplained noises throughout the building, like the sound of cowboy boots walking across the floor. The noises were followed by claims that people had heard a bodiless voice emanate from the shadows, whispering their names. Soon there were actual sightings of the phantom. He was invariably described as a tall, lanky cowboy in dusty, but well-tailored, western-style clothes. Glimpses of the spirit were often so brief that it took some time before it was identified as Bullock's, but when the connection was made it soon became obvious that it couldn't be anyone else's.

Today guests can speak to the late sheriff through a descendent of his named Sandy Bullock. A psychic, Sandy has mastered the ability to contact his distant relation and relate his feelings to anyone interested enough to ask. Sandy helped to determine, for instance, that Bullock seemed strangely apprehensive about the restoration of his hotel at first, but he quickly changed his mind and began to enjoy the constant company it afforded.

There is even one recorded incident in which Bullock's spirit came to the aid of a lost little boy. According to Ken Gienger, a former manager at the hotel, a young boy left his room to find his father who was gambling in the hotel's gaming hall. The hotel's halls, though, proved too circuitous for the boy and he quickly became lost. Alone and afraid, he started to cry. His sobs brought him to the attention of a tall stranger.

The historic Bullock Hotel in Deadwood, South Dakota

"Hush now, boy. What's with the alligator tears?" the stranger asked.

The boy told the man, whose clothes were strangely out of date, that he was lost.

"Well, that's no reason to blubber like that. Not for a big boy like you."

Chastened, the boy stopped crying.

"Now don't worry," the stranger continued. "I know this place like the back of my hand. What room are you staying at?"

The boy told him.

"Well, there you go!" the stranger laughed. "That's only down the hall from here. Come on and follow me and I'll show you."

The stranger was right. The boy had gotten so disoriented that he had failed to notice how close he was to his room.

"There you are." The stranger smiled as they arrived at the boy's door. He crouched down and looked the grateful boy in the eye. "Now I want you to promise me that you'll be more careful walking through these halls. There's nothing I hate more than seeing a strong little boy like yourself bawling like a baby."

The boy promised the stranger that he'd be more careful and the tall man smiled, tousled the boy's hair and walked away. When his father finally came back from the gaming hall, the boy told him about his getting lost and of the nice man who helped him. It was only as the two were checking out that the identity of the stranger became clear. The father was at the front desk paying the bill when the boy noticed a picture that hung above the lobby's couch. He immediately recognized the man in it and excitedly tugged on his father's jacket.

"Dad!" he breathlessly exclaimed.

"What?" his father replied, annoyed by the interruption.

"That's the man who helped me!" The boy pointed to the photograph.

The boy's father looked at the picture and nearly fainted when he realized his son had been helped by the hotel's famous phantom.

In 1964 Deadwood became the first American town to be declared a historical landmark by the federal government. This honor might never have been bestowed were it not for the efforts of its first protector, Seth Bullock. One of the great men of his time, he ensured that the small town with the hard-to-forget name was not consumed by the lawlessness of the era. In fact, the town flourished throughout the past century. Perhaps, then, it is pride that keeps Bullock at the hotel that bears his name. His spirit knows that few men have been fortunate enough to leave such a positive legacy in the world. His reward is the knowledge that his impact has not been forgotten.

Hot Water
CHICO, MONTANA

Sometimes an occurrence that is completely natural takes on the air of the paranormal because it is so antithetical to what people commonly assume is the natural order. Consider hot springs, those warm pools of water that require no human aid to keep their temperatures up. It isn't hard to believe that back when such springs were first discovered, many people were terrified that the water was warmed by the very flames of Hell and that entering the water meant risking damnation.

The belief that the waters were warmed by fires inside the earth is not inaccurate. The flames in question, however, originate in the planet's hot magma core and not in a pit of never-ending torment. Eventually skeptics overcame this superstitious fear and people began to associate the comfort of soaking in a hot spring with a therapeutic effect. As a result, many of the springs were bought by entrepreneurs who built spas and resorts around them, hoping that people would be willing to pay for the opportunity to relax in the warm water. Their hopes bore fruit and people flocked to the different springs.

In 1876, a spring was discovered in the rural Montana area known as Chico. (When the government insisted the sparsely populated zone be given a name for mail purposes, the residents named it after a friendly and talkative Hispanic miner.) Two decades later, the land on which the spring sat came to be owned by Bill and Percie Knowles.

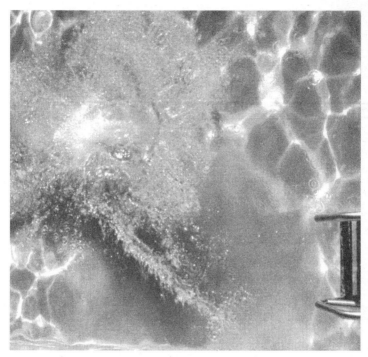

Before their therapeutic value was determined, hot springs were believed to have a supernatural, even diabolical, source.

At first they had little use for the warm water, so they used the property to operate a boardinghouse for miners. But when they began to see advertisements for a variety of spas and resorts around the country, the pair realized they were sitting on a gold mine of sorts.

In 1900, the couple opened the Chico Warm Springs Hotel and promoted it as a place to cure rheumatism, stomach and kidney troubles and skin and blood diseases. Being of two very different temperaments, Bill and Percie disagreed on the true purpose of the hotel. Percie wanted it to be a place where sick people came to get well, while her husband was happier making it a place where visitors could come and have a good time. To this end, he built a dance hall and a saloon—a move that Percie, a lifelong teetotaler, vehemently opposed.

In the end Percie may have had a point, because ten years after the couple opened the hotel, Bill died from cirrhosis of the liver, having enjoyed a few too many drinks in his beloved saloon. Almost immediately after his death, Percie closed down the saloon and, along with her 12-year-old son Radbourne, set about bringing her vision of the hotel to fruition. She hired a doctor named George A. Townsend and with his help turned the hotel into a first-rate hospital that gained renown throughout the northwest. After Dr. Townsend retired in 1925, the hospital's reputation began to fade until it finally closed down in 1943, owing to Radbourne's death at the age of 45. Over the next 30 years, a variety of different owners operated the hotel, each having his or her own ideas of what it should be. One owner tried to turn the hotel into a casino, while another turned it into a dude ranch. The hotel expanded under the different owners and grew to become a resort.

Mike and Eve Art, a couple from Ohio, bought the resort in 1973, seeing in it a connection to the past. They decided to restore it to the way it looked when Bill and Percie first opened it. The Arts recaptured the hotel's original Georgian-inspired architecture and Craftsman-style interiors and furnished it with period antiques. They called the structure the Chico Hot Springs Resort, and for the past three decades it has remained so. The resort now consists of the original hotel, a series of private cabins, two pools, two restaurants, a gift shop, an activity center, a convention facility, a horse barn and—in a sign that the Arts' aspirations are closer to Bill's than Percie's—a saloon.

While evidence of paranormal activity had been first noticed at the resort as early as 1967, it wasn't until the Arts took over that the strange incidents began to occur with any frequency. Like Sheriff Bullock at the Bullock Hotel in Deadwood, South Dakota, Brigham Young in Salt Lake City, Utah, and the different ghosts at the Molly Brown House in Denver, Colorado, it appeared that the restoration of the Chico Hot Springs Resort resurrected not only the hotel's fortunes, but also the ghost of one of its original owners.

Percie Knowles died alone in a room in the Warm-springs State Hospital in 1941. The stress of running a business on her own had proven to be too much for the frail woman to endure. Knowing that the springs weren't equipped to handle his mother's physical and mental decline, Radbourne Knowles sent her to the state hospital in 1936 with little hope that she would ever recover.

Never a large woman, Percie resembled a malnourished bird at the time of her death, her bones clearly visible under her wrinkled, translucent skin. She was buried wearing her favorite white dress—an outfit by which she would later be recognized when her ghost began manifesting itself throughout the hotel. It is clear that the resort meant everything to her, and its failure resulted in a breakdown that eventually ended her life. It isn't shocking, then, that when the resort finally found itself successful once again, she would return so she could bask in the glory of what she and her husband had started.

While people on staff at the resort were familiar with the odd noises and strange happenings that had become commonplace at the hotel, it wasn't until 1986 that they encountered a full-on apparition. It was late at night on a Sunday in May. Two security guards, Tim Barnes and Ron Woolery, had just returned to the hotel after closing up the saloon when Tim spotted something near the lobby's piano. He turned towards the piano to get a better look and froze where he stood. His mouth dropped open as he stared in bewildered amazement.

"Uh..." was all he managed to say as he tapped his partner on the arm.

"What?" Ron turned and was also rendered speechless by what he saw.

There, floating above the piano, was a smoky transparent figure of a person. The ghost's head, body and arms were fully formed, but below its waist there was only a shapeless white mass that had the appearance of a long flowing skirt. The phantom's face was neither clearly male nor female and it bore no sign of emotion. The two guards had no idea if it was good or evil. A few seconds that felt like minutes passed before Ron and Tim were capable of rational thought.

"You don't see something like this everyday," Tim remarked.

"Nope," Ron agreed.

"In fact, I bet we won't ever see something like this again."

"Nope."

"And I'm sure that no one will believe us when we say that we did."

"Nope."

"We should take a picture so people won't think we're crazy. I happen to know that there's a Polaroid camera in the office. Do you want to go get it?"

"Nope."

Tim understood why Ron was reluctant. The office was right next to the piano, and gaining access to it required coming within just a few feet of the spirit's grasp. Still, sensing that this could be his moment of glory, Tim dashed towards the office door and managed to open it and get inside. The effort winded him and he puffed and gasped as he searched for the camera, which he had seen another staff member use during a party for the guests. He found it, but in his haste he forgot to grab the flash cubes that sat next to it.

With all his remaining energy, Tim dashed back to Ron and used the last remaining photo in the Polaroid's cartridge to snap a picture. As soon as the camera spit out the photograph, the ghost dispersed as if it had been hit by a heavy wind. Ron and Tim waited for the photograph to develop. Unfortunately, without the flash the result was disappointing. All that was visible was a tiny white spot that bore little resemblance to the floating figure they had encountered.

Despite the setback, Ron's fear that he and his partner would not be believed proved unwarranted when a host of other staff members began to see the same spirit. Among those who joined the two security guards in becoming ardent believers were Tim's mother, Edie Mundall, who worked at the hotel as a night auditor; Terrie Angell, one of the hotel's bartenders; and a maid named Lindy

The Chico Hot Springs Resort in Montana, home to the ghost of Percie Knowles

Moore, who was one of the first to suggest that the ghost was Percie Knowles. Each described the ghost in much the same way that Ron and Tim did after their first encounter.

Over the years that followed, it became clear that the one place where a guest or employee would most likely come in contact with the spirit was room 349, which, coincidentally, was the room in which Percie stayed during her last years at the hotel. The spirit's connection to that room became clear when security guards noticed that no matter how many times they locked it during their shifts, it was always open when they returned. As well, staff members noticed how an antique rocking chair in the room could frequently be seen rocking all by itself, although the windows were closed and the room was free from drafts.

More eerie evidence of Percie's supernatural return from the grave can be found in the hotel's attic, which contains a bible once owned by the Knowleses. Much to the disbelief of the hotel's staff, this particular bible—which has always been found sitting open on the same page of Psalms—has never once become dusty, despite the long periods in which it goes untouched. As well, curious staff members have tried closing the book and leaving it open on a different page, only to find that the book's open pages invariably return to the original pages.

Percie can also be heard in the hotel's kitchen, where she often bangs loudly on pots and pans and breaks the occasional dish. On other occasions, Percie has managed to light candles in the kitchen and has been heard moaning throughout the hallways. She can be something of a trickster, moving or stealing objects from the employees just when they need them. This uncharacteristic habit of practical jokery has caused some to theorize that the mental distress that led to her hospitalization has left her ghost giddy and unstable. Others have suggested that Percie's ghost has reverted back to the girl she was at the age of 12. Those who believe the latter possibility have claimed that Percie's presence has an aura that is distinctly childlike. Given that Percie's childhood was one of the happiest periods of her life, this idea isn't far-fetched.

It is interesting that two of the few places that have not been settings for Percie's visits are the pools for which the hotel was created. Untreated by any chemicals, these naturally warm pools are in a way every bit as wondrous as the hotel's famous phantom. Although they can be easily explained by science, they still manage to seem inexplicable, proving that, when it wants to, the natural can fire the imagination just as much as the supernatural. The Chico Hot Springs Resort, therefore, is doubly blessed— both by the beauty of the earthbound and the miraculously metaphysical. Designed to be a place where people can relax and forget their troubles, it does just that, reminding all who stay there that no matter how much you think you have it figured out, the world can always surprise you.

3
Ghosts of the Frontier

Burnt Black and Frozen Blue
RIDGEWAY, WISCONSIN

It was a bone-chilling winter night in 1840 when two teenage boys walked into McKillip's Saloon, a dirty shack just five miles east of the small town of Ridgeway, Wisconsin. With the same dark black hair and steely blue eyes, the pair looked to be brothers, although one was slightly taller than the other. The tall one looked to be about 15, while the other one looked about a year younger. Their clothes were worn and ill-suited for the freezing conditions outside. Their faces were frostbitten and their bodies shivered uncontrollably. They walked as fast as they could to the saloon's fireplace and sighed with relief when they felt its heat.

"I was so cold I thought I would die," whispered the older boy to his brother.

"I was so cold I thought I was dead," his brother whispered back.

"Hoy!" shouted McKillip, the tavern's owner, a short fat man. "That fire's not for free. Order something or get out!"

The two boys looked at each other worriedly. The older boy took out a small bag from his pocket. It was nearly empty. The change it held would be just enough to buy two drinks.

"We'll have no more money," the older boy informed his brother.

"I'd rather be warm and busted than freezing to death with a few pennies in my pocket."

The older boy nodded and used the last of their money to buy a couple cups of coffee. They drank it as slowly as they could. As they did, they warmed up enough to look away from the flames and get a sense of where they actually were. Their eyes widened as they took in the sight of scarred, fierce-looking clientele. The younger boy made the mistake of making eye contact with a large bald man whose head was short one ear.

"What are you looking at?" the large man growled, his words made somewhat incomprehensible by his mouth's absence of teeth. The force with which he spoke, however, was enough for his meaning to be immediately clear.

"Nothing. I'm sorry."

"Did you just call me nothing?" the man sneered.

"No! I just meant I wasn't looking at anything." The boy's voice trembled with fear.

"We don't take kindly to liars, boy," warned a grizzled man whose missing left eye bore no patch. "I saw you staring at my friend."

"I wasn't staring!" the boy insisted.

"Why? I too ugly to look at? Do I make you sick?" the bald man asked with a sadistic gleam in his eye.

"No! You're not ugly. You're as handsome as anybody."

The men in the bar roared with laughter.

"I think you've got an admirer," teased a voice from the back.

"That's not what I meant," the boy tried to explain.

The boy's brother had had enough of this.

"Leave him alone," he ordered the crowd, realizing as he spoke that his words were probably going to make things worse.

The bar grew silent. The bald man walked over to the older brother and looked down into his eyes.

"Who are you to tell us what to do?" the man asked.

The boy stayed quiet while his younger brother pleaded to the large man.

"We'll leave right now, sir. We don't want any trouble."

The bald man turned his head to the younger boy and smiled wickedly.

"But I do."

With that he threw his forehead into the older boy's face. The boy screamed with pain as blood spurted out of his nose. Before he could defend himself, his attacker punched him in the stomach and kneed him in the face when he doubled over. The other men in the bar laughed and cheered the bald man on. He turned to them and took a bow. While he showboated, his victim managed to stand. He grabbed a mug from a nearby table. He smashed it against the back of the man's head. The man screamed with rage and turned back towards the boy. A murderous hatred shone in his eyes as he lifted the boy up and threw him into the fireplace.

Shocked beyond speech, the younger boy watched as his brother wailed and screamed from the pain. His clothes were overtaken by the flames.

"Now he's warm enough," exclaimed a cruel voice from the back.

The bald man turned towards the younger boy, who for a moment was too horrified to consider that he was still in danger himself. He had covered his ears to save himself from his brother's screams and had closed his eyes so he couldn't see the all-consuming power of the flames.

But when he felt the bald man's hand on the back of his neck, his survival instinct kicked in. He jumped up and managed to free himself of the bald man's grasp. He ran through the tangle of men, avoiding their arms and legs as he made his way to the door. Just as he got to it a hand grabbed at his coat. He slipped out of it and ran out of the saloon as fast as his feet could manage.

Several days later, his lifeless body was found in a field. He had escaped the hell of the tavern's fire only to freeze to death outside. No one ever found out who the boys were or why they were out alone on that cold night. Over the years that followed, many people had the opportunity to ask the boys themselves, but the sensation of overwhelming terror made those questions hard to pose.

From 1840 to 1910, the ghosts of those two murdered boys haunted the crossroads of Ridgeway. During those years the people who lived there seldom walked or rode without an escort. The boys craved vengeance and lacked the patience to distinguish between the guilty and the innocent. Those they attacked at night had little chance of survival.

The pair would appear to unwary travelers in a variety of shapes, both human and animal. Sometimes they were a pack of dogs, a carriage of horses or a herd of pigs. On other occasions, they appeared as headless men, young and old women and as themselves, burnt black and frozen blue. They took whatever shape they felt would be most effective in any given situation. Once the older brother attacked a man as a ball of white-hot flame. His victim had the misfortune of being bald.

Despite the frequency of the brothers' attacks, there were still some in Ridgeway who dismissed the wraiths as superstitious nonsense. One of these skeptics was a mountain of a man named Even Lewis. A butcher by trade, Even was famous around the state as a champion wrestler. His massive bulk allowed him to cut through bone and meat as easily as it allowed him to pin anyone who wrestled him. He was nicknamed the Strangler because of his fondness for choke holds. He was not a man who was easily intimidated. Fear to him was something other people experienced, usually when he walked into a room. Along with his muscles, Even's confidence was further strengthened by the knives he carried as part of his trade. People could talk about ghosts all they wanted; they weren't going to stop him from walking home at night. Only a fool, living or dead, would make the mistake of trying to attack him.

On May 6, 1874, Even was halfway across a large pasture when he felt the warmth of a stranger's breath on his right hand. As he turned he heard the sound of a low, threatening growl. A large breedless black dog with teeth as sharp and menacing as the knives Even carried stood close enough to him to tear out his neck. What shocked Even the most were the dog's eyes. They were blue and they looked at him with the intelligence of a man. The dog's growl grew louder and drool began to drip from its teeth.

"Nice doggy," was all Even could think of to say.

The dog's growl erupted into an apocalyptic bark and Even dropped his knives and ran as the infernal beast bit at his heals. Even was not used to running. The strain of his great weight caused his lungs to gasp for air. He ran until he thought they would burst and then, knowing he had no choice but to stop, he turned suddenly and kicked the dog with all his might. His foot passed through it like it was a wisp of smoke. The force of his kick threw him from his feet and he crashed painfully on his back.

The dog vanished and Even spent an hour on the ground before he had the strength to move. He was only a short distance from the cabin he shared with his wife and children, but it took him hours to get there. When he finally reached it, he collapsed at the door. Somehow his family was able to lift him up and get him into bed, where he told them of what had happened to him. Two days later, his heart, weakened by the strain he had put it through, finally gave up on him. He died in bed.

In 1910 a fire broke out in Ridgeway and turned most of the town into ash. A rumor soon took hold that the two angry spirits were seen in the window of a burning building with content smiles on their faces. Whether or not the two boys were responsible for the fire has never been proven. What is known is that after the fire they were never seen on Ridgeway's roads again.

Comstock's Mine
VIRGINIA CITY, NEVADA

In 1859, three simple men—Patrick McLaughlin, Peter O'Reilly and Henry Comstock—happened upon what would become the single richest silver strike in history. Either unaware of what they had come across or simply too greedy to reject the quick cash that was dangled in front of them, each sold his share of the mine for a ludicrously insignificant fraction of what it was worth. All three could have been millionaires many times over, but instead they died miserable and penniless, despairing over the failure to take hold of the one great opportunity life had given them. And, as the following story shows, at least one of them would continue to wallow in this misery long after his death.

The discovery resulted in a mass migration of prospectors, schemers and others to the area (in present-day Nevada). The hopefuls gathered together in a small town made up of tents and dugouts. It was named "Old Virginny" after a drunken prospector named James Finney christened the ground one night with a bottle of whiskey. As more and more people flooded into the area, Old Virginny became Virginia City, a boomtown where a man could arrive penniless and leave wealthy. Among the fortune-seekers was a man named Samuel Clemens. He wrote for the local newspaper, which did little more than serve as an advertisement for the mining industry. Only later did he achieve fame under the pen name of Mark Twain.

Thanks to the wealth created by the mine, the territory of Nevada became important to the federal government during the Civil War. The cost of the war was dragging the treasury toward bankruptcy, and President Lincoln—knowing that the gold and silver being mined in Virginia City would help the government remain solvent—made Nevada a state, despite its having too small a population to qualify constitutionally.

As is the case with many former gold rush cities, Virginia City today relies on its past to keep afloat. With the mines now closed, tourism is the city's main industry. People come from all around to see the city that was, in its heyday, called "the Richest Place on Earth."

To the three men most responsible for the creation of Virginia City and the wealth that it brought, that nickname must have been a very bitter pill to swallow. The discovery of the mine was truly an accident. Peter and Patrick, two prospectors who were known to team up on occasion, were digging a ditch to collect water when they found a layer of soil that glistened in the sun. At long last, they had uncovered the strike they had spent their lives searching for.

Just as they made their discovery, though, Henry Comstock, another prospector, rode into their camp and saw what the two men had discovered. He insisted that the find was located on his land; Peter and Patrick were gullible enough to believe him. To appease him, the two men offered him a partnership, which Henry accepted on the spot. They decided to call their discovery the Ophir Mine, but on account of Henry's incorrigible braggadocio it was soon labeled the Comstock Lode by everyone who talked about it.

In the weeks following the strike, another miner—a man named Stone—determined that the gold mine that the three men described was actually far richer in silver. In fact, it was the single largest vein of silver ever found. As in many stories from this get-rich-quick era, all three men sold their shares before the true value of the strike became evident. Henry was paid $11,500 for his share. Had he kept it, it would have brought him about $80 million more (which would have made him one of the wealthiest men on the planet). Patrick fared even worse than Henry, selling his share for a mere $3500. The sum was more money than he had ever seen in his life, but in the end it was only a tiny percentage of the strike's value. Peter was the shrewdest of the three. He waited until he was offered $50,000 for his share before he sold it.

Each man would end up greatly regretting his hastiness. Eleven years after selling his shares, Henry shot himself in the head. Patrick went broke soon after receiving his money and ended up working odd jobs for the rest of his life. Peter became an alcoholic and lost his sanity in a gin-soaked haze. He died in a straightjacket. Although each had cause to haunt the mine, only one of them returned to make his bitter presence felt in ghostly form.

One winter night, an unearthly light shot up out of one of the shafts of the mine and 60 feet into the air. Since it was visible for miles around, the residents of nearby Virginia City assumed it was a fire and decided to stop it before it began to spread. When they arrived, they discovered that there wasn't even the remotest hint of flames. The light still shone, but there was no explanation for it. A few brave souls stuck their heads into the shaft and reported that they heard the sounds of a pickax breaking rock several hundred feet below. That area of the mine had been long deserted and no one could think of anyone who would go down there, especially at night. As the bewildered locals pondered the mystery, the light began to fade and the sounds stopped. Scratching their heads, everyone went home.

The next day the inexplicable activity recurred. The first incident involved the mine's elevator operator, who was surprised when he got a signal asking him to send the elevator down to the abandoned 700-foot level. Then another signal instructed him to take the elevator down one more level, followed by a signal to return to the surface. When the caged elevator resurfaced, the operator was shocked to discover that it was empty.

As the days passed, the miners began to report hearing bizarre sounds coming from the 700-foot level. Besides the sound of a phantom pickax, they also heard the sound of a horrible deep-throated laugh. The men began to talk about sending down a search party to investigate, but it became clear that no one was too keen to join up.

Frank Kennedy, a young man with all the confidence in the world, was amused by the cowardice of his co-workers.

"You call yourselves miners? You guys face death a thousand different ways each day and you're scared of a few noises!"

"I don't see you volunteerin'!" shot back an offended cohort.

"Just because I don't believe in wasting time with fairy tales," Frank retorted. "But if you're all going make a big a big deal out of it, then I'll go. There can't be anything down there that I haven't seen up here."

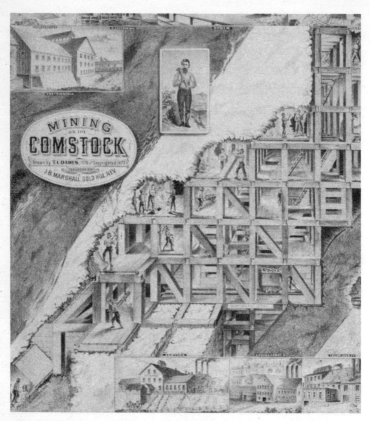

Plan of the Comstock Mine, Virginia City, Nevada

There was a smirk on Frank's face as the elevator descended down to the 700-foot level. When the elevator stopped and he got out, there was a distinct cockiness in his swagger. Frank knew these mines as well as anybody and he knew there was nothing in them a careful person should be scared of. The only thing a person had to worry about was keeping track of where they were going. The tunnels in the mine ran for miles and an accidental wrong turn could result in sudden disorientation. Frank made sure to keep going straight down the main tunnel. He concentrated so hard on keeping his bearings that he failed at first to notice the distant sound of a pickax breaking rock.

He had walked a full mile through the tunnel when he finally noticed the sound. For the first time Frank began to worry that he might not be alone. His heart began to pound and his breathing grew heavy. He knew that the sound was coming from a spot where no miner had stood for years. It was only the fear of his co-workers' mockery that kept him from running back to the elevator. It took him a minute to convince himself that there had to be some rational explanation for the sounds. He calmed down and started moving towards the noise, eager to make a discovery that would disprove the superstitious fears of his fellow miners.

As he walked, the sound of the pickax grew louder and steadier with each step. His composure vanished when he heard the sound of a man laughing. This time Frank turned back and began to run, but again the fear of being thought a coward proved even greater incentive than the possibility of what lay ahead. He clenched his fists, gritted his teeth, turned back around and made his way towards the sounds. The blood began to race through his body so fast that the rushing sound it created in his head almost drowned out the spine-chilling noises he was following. The fear turned his face blood red. Another miner coming upon him probably would have been as frightened by Frank as by the unexplained sounds. Finally he reached a turn in the tunnel. It was clear that whoever was making the sounds was on the other side of it. Frank summoned up every ounce of courage and rounded the corner.

What he saw froze him in his tracks. There, tapping away at the rock with a pickax, he saw the corpse of a man he had once seen in a picture. Surrounded by an aura of silver light, the dead man turned to Frank and spoke to him.

"Do you know who I am?" The ghost's voice was hollow, as if the sound did not come from his mouth but his entire body.

Somehow Frank was able to answer him, although with barely a whisper.

"You're…you're…Henry Comstock."

"That's right." The ghost leaned in towards Frank. Its rotting face hung loosely from its skull, with eyes the color of bile and pupils that danced like blue flames. A hole was visible at the back of its head, a gruesome reminder of the bullet with which Comstock took his own life. "I'm Henry Comstock and this is MY MINE! You hear? MINE!"

Then the ghost raised his pickax and moved towards Frank, who turned and ran as fast as he had ever run in his life. He ran and ran, not once turning around to see if he was being followed. He finally reached the elevator, slammed it shut and signaled frantically for it to be brought back up to the surface.

For a long time no amount of coaxing could get Frank to tell anyone his story, and when he finally did many refused to believe it. Locals assumed he was just having fun at their expense for being so scared themselves, but it soon became clear that Frank would sooner die than return to the 700-foot level.

Those who clung to their skepticism abandoned it when a mysterious force took to blowing out the candles used in the mine. The elevator, no less, was often called to descend to levels where no one was working. In these deserted areas, the sound of Henry's laughter could be heard reverberating through the tunnels.

Henry Comstock was not the only man whose hopes were shattered during the gold rush. One of the defining characteristics of the period was the winning and losing of fortunes by men who mistakenly believed that their good luck would last forever. It almost never did. People came from all over to Virginia City with dreams of incredible wealth. Many saw those dreams become nightmares, but few came as close as Henry did to true greatness. Had he not been so greedy, he could have become an incredibly rich and powerful man. Perhaps that is why his ghost is so loath to give up the mine that bears his name.

The McLoughlin House
OREGON CITY, OREGON

On a hilltop in Oregon City, Oregon, one of the city's oldest houses serves as a museum dedicated to the city's past. The McLoughlin House was home to Dr. John McLoughlin from 1846 to his death in 1857. Starting out as a doctor, McLoughlin eventually became a prominent employee of the famous Hudson's Bay Company. He was instrumental in the creation not only of Oregon City, but also of the state of Oregon. He served as mayor of the city and was also its greatest single benefactor. Following his death, the house was moved from where it originally stood, as were the graves of Dr. McLoughlin and his wife, Marguerite. After this relocation, the house began to play host to a number of supernatural occurrences—a fact that suggests that not everyone was happy to have a new view.

By all accounts, Dr. McLoughlin was a very tall and imposing man. Standing 6'5" with a shoulder-length mane of snow-white hair, even when he was alive he was almost a humorous cliché of a stern phantom with hypnotic eyes. McLoughlin was born in the Canadian province of Quebec in 1784, and as the nephew of the explorer Simon Fraser, the young Dr. McLoughlin became involved in the fur trade. He was soon appointed as the chief medical office for the North West Company, one of two fiercely competitive North American fur-trading outfits.

The shocking whiteness of Dr. McLoughlin's hair came as a result of a skirmish between his employers and their rivals, the Hudson's Bay Company. In the midst of a zone war between the two, Dr. McLoughlin gallantly accepted the blame for an unfortunate incident, in spite of his own innocence. He was arrested and sent out on a canoe on Lake Superior, on the other side of which his trial was to take place. He and his captors were met halfway through their journey by a wave that upturned the canoe. The others drowned in the icy water, but Dr. McLoughlin managed to survive. The ordeal was so traumatic that his hair turned white and never regained its color.

McLoughlin was soon cleared of the murder charge, and when the two rival companies decided to boost their fortunes through a merger, he was one of 25 men named as chief factors. He was appointed the head of operations at Fort Vancouver, where, because of his great generosity, he soon became a much-loved and respected figure. Ironically, his generosity led to his termination from the Hudson's Bay Company. The company wanted to keep the territory as sparsely populated as possible, but settlers soon began arriving by the hundreds. The majority of these men, women and children arrived sick, hungry and without any of the supplies necessary for survival. The company's policy was to let them starve— an act of indifference that horrified Dr. McLoughlin. Instead, he defied his orders and gave aid to the settlers. Not long after, he was forced to resign for his compassionate acts.

Looking for a place to spend his retirement, McLoughlin bought a parcel of land near Willamette Falls. He paid workers to clear and develop the area, erected several public buildings on it and built a house for himself and his family.

The McLoughlin House, Oregon City, Oregon

In spite of his magnanimity, many resented his wealth and deplored the fact that he was still a Canadian citizen.

Not long after Oregon was granted statehood, a conspiracy developed to rob Dr. McLoughlin of his land. He tried to counteract this by applying for American citizenship, but his efforts proved futile and his land became the property of the state. The stress of the legal battle proved too much for the good doctor. Bitter and heartbroken, he died in his home, which those who had conspired against him had so generously allowed him to keep.

After his death, his house was sold and served as a camp for Chinese laborers, a brothel, a hotel and an apartment before it was moved to its current location and turned into a museum. Because so many different people lived and died in the house, the ghosts that reside within are greatly varied in nature.

The most famous of the museum's ghosts is Dr. McLoughlin himself. Seen as a shadow walking heavily through the house's halls, he still has to duck when passing through a doorway. Above the house's large fireplace, an oil painting in his image takes on a strange iridescent glow when the sun hits it every September 3 at 9:35 in the morning. The most bizarre of the tales, however, involves a curator at the museum who repeatedly found that his change was being stolen from him. Eventually the money was found in a locked drawer to which the curator had the only key. While he found the incident more than a bit curious, he did not dwell on it. It was only through some completely unrelated research that he discovered that there might be an unearthly reason for the petty thievery.

During his research, the curator discovered that a descendant of his had been given a substantial loan by the charitable Dr. McLoughlin but had failed to pay back the final $43 that she owed. Fully aware of the shadowy figure lurking through the halls, the curator couldn't help but wonder if the ghost was just trying to get his money back.

Another well-known ghost at the museum is Dr. McLoughlin's wife, Marguerite, a beautiful woman of Cree and Swedish heritage. Her presence is most often accompanied by the smell of pipe tobacco in the air. In her later years, Marguerite was seldom without her pipe. In some cases, the odor has been known to follow people as they move throughout the house, as if Marguerite is checking up on them and seeing that they are doing a good job.

Over the years there have been a number of other paranormal sightings and occurrences in the McLoughlin House. Some have been connected to the original owners, while others are most likely remnants of the house's colorful past. Among the ghosts sensed by visiting psychics is the protective spirit of an Indian servant who served under the McLoughlins and the disturbed ghost of a man who died inside the house during a failed amputation (Dr. McLoughlin practiced medicine when emergencies required it).

One visitor wasn't surprised to learn that the house was once a labor camp for Chinese railroad workers, since she had reported seeing a group of terrified Chinese ghosts huddled together in a room. History indicates that the Chinese workers who lived in the house did not leave it voluntarily, but were instead forced out by a gang of racist townspeople. This seems a good explanation for their fear. Yet another ghost, seen by several visitors, serves as a reminder of the house's tenure as a brothel. Dressed in a beautiful period gown, this ghost languidly walks down the staircase with a seductive come-hither look on her face, trolling for a prospective customer.

Dr. McLoughlin's house has become more than a simple museum; it is also a spiritual place. The ghosts within serve as better reminders of the past than any antiques and plaques ever could. After all, it is much harder to make an emotional connection to a piece of furniture than to the spirit of the person who once owned it. Dr. McLoughlin's house is proof of this theory. His stories, as well as those of his wife and others, elevate the museum from a mere tourist attraction into a place where people can go and feel a connection to history so elusive anywhere else.

Forest Farm House
SALT LAKE CITY, UTAH

Salt Lake City, Utah, is home to a living museum dedicated to the state's past. Known as the Old Desert Group, the museum is made up of a collection of the first homes to be built in the city. The homes, which have been moved from their original locations, have been completely restored. Dressed in historical garb, park employees give tours demonstrating the way of life of the brave men and women who first lived in the buildings. The most important of these buildings is known as Forest Farm House. Built around 1850 by Salt Lake City's founder, Brigham Young, the house has become a rich spiritual document of the era.

From 1839 to 1846, the town of Nauvoo, Illinois, was the home of the Mormon Church. Founded by Joseph Smith, the church (which is also known as the Church of Jesus Christ of Latter-day Saints) saw its membership rise dramatically during those years. But the gentile population of Illinois was offended by the church's practice of polygamy and were frightened by the large, well-armed

Mormon pioneer Brigham Young, circa 1866

militia it had formed. By 1844, their paranoia grew into violence when Smith and his brother Hyrum were killed by an angry mob. Brigham Young replaced the murdered leader and wisely made plans to move his flock—some 11,000 followers—to a place where they would not have to deal with intolerance.

The group left Nauvoo on February 4, 1846. They reached the Missouri River at the end of the first part of their trek, but it took them four months to travel 265 miles. After several camps were established, Young and 147 other settlers formed a lead pioneer party that started the second part of the journey on April 5, 1847. Much better organized on this second part of the trek, the group traveled almost five times the distance in the same amount of time, covering 1032 miles in four months. On July 24, 1847, the first pioneers entered the Valley of the Great Salt Lake. As soon as they arrived, they began to plant crops, build shelter and welcome the other settlers who followed them. By the time winter arrived, 1650 people were living in what would become Salt Lake City, a settlement that would result in the creation of the state of Utah.

Once the city had been established, Young set about building several homes for himself and his many wives. The main house, in which he would live, was Forest Farm House, a two-story, wooden gabled structure whose porch wrapped all the way around the building. By the time the house was completed, Young had 18 wives who intermittently lived in the main house and surrounding satellite buildings. Young lived there until his death in 1877. Thirteen years later, polygamy was outlawed by the church to make Utah eligible for statehood. Over the years that followed, the house went through several hands. In the 1950s it was bought by an antiques dealer and noted psychic named Gwen Wilcox, who, along with her husband, was intent on restoring the historic building.

Gwen's psychic abilities were authenticated when she used them to successfully aid the investigations of the local police force. It was because of her ability that six weeks after moving in she began to make contact with the house's spirits. The first ghost she came across was that of a 75-year-old man. She found him in the front room, sitting in a chair with his feet propped up on a stool and a cane in his hand. Gwen recognized him right away.

"Hello, Mr. Young." She spoke to him using her psychic ability.

"Hello, Mrs. Wilcox," he greeted her back.

In the following years, Brigham Young's ghost frequently visited the Wilcoxes and gave them useful information that helped them with the house's restoration. Always friendly and sociable, he was a welcome relief compared to the dark wraith that always brought a frightening chill to any room it entered. This angry shadow was the ghost of a thief who had murdered someone during an attempted robbery down the street from the house. A tortured soul, he appeared infrequently, but when he did Gwen and her family would quickly leave the room.

It took 15 years for Gwen and her husband to complete Forest Farm House's renovation. When they did, they donated the house to the Mormon Church. To celebrate this act of generosity, the church held a celebration at the house in the Wilcoxes' honor. During the party, Gwen and her husband met a handsome young man, who, like the other guests, had dressed in period clothing. They chatted and were pleasantly surprised by the young man's historical knowledge of the house. Another guest saw the three chatting and took a photograph of them together. Everyone was shocked when the picture was developed and only the Wilcoxes appeared in it. The space where the young man had stood was empty. This spirit's appearance was so lifelike that even a gifted psychic like

Gwen had no idea he was a ghost. While the identity of this phantom party guest is still unknown, many believe he was John Young, Brigham Young's favorite son.

After the house was donated to the church, the decision was made to move it to Pioneer State Trail Park where it would become the centerpiece of the Old Desert Group. The ghost of Brigham Young, overjoyed to see his house restored to its former glory, passed on and did not travel with the house to its new location. The dark spirit also moved out, wanting to keep close to the scene of its crime. However, this development did not mean the end of supernatural guests taking the time to visit the historic home.

The most well known of Forest Farm's current ghosts is Ann Eliza Webb, who was the 27th woman to marry Brigham Young. Ann, 23 to Young's 66, was a young firecracker who bridled at her status as Young's 19th wife (as he had 18 other living wives at the time of their marriage). She quickly discovered that she despised the subtle pecking order and petty treacheries that came with the arrangement. She especially seemed to hate Forest Farm House and despaired whenever it was her turn to occupy it. Her hatred of the house seemed largely arbitrary, focusing mostly on the trivial matter of the house's living room staircase. She so hated the design of the house that when it was recreated in the townhouse Young built for her, she divorced him rather than live in it. She then wrote a book about her life with the Mormon leader. Entitled *Wife #19: The Story of a Life in Bondage,* it was filled with angry attacks denouncing the Mormon faith.

Despite her hatred of the house, something in recent years has drawn Ann back to it. What exactly is a matter

Ann Young, a reluctant wife of Brigham Young, haunts the home where she once lived.

of much speculation. Some believe it is her punishment for attacking the church, while others believe that she has come back to search for the peace that eluded her during her life. Either way, none of her appearances are indicative of a typical unhappy spirit.

The first time she was spotted was at the birthday party of one of the house's tour guides. Three guests were talking in the kitchen when two of them saw Ann's easily recognizable figure looking at them through a window. On another occasion, she caused a bit of spiritual razzle-dazzle during a routine tour. When the tour guide pointed out a wreath made by Young's wives out of their own hair, Ann, who was invisible at the time, lifted it up and held it out to them. When the guide finished her prepared speech, Ann put it back on the nail on which it was hung and left the witnesses with their mouths hanging open.

Two other bizarre events that have occurred frequently over the years are the sound of invisible children at play in the house and the smell of homemade chicken soup coming from the kitchen. Children have been heard during the months when the Old Desert Group is closed to visitors and thus lacking the echoes of young visitors who frequent the house during the tourist season. As for the smell of soup, the assumption is that it is the result of the tour guides making their lunch, but since the kitchen doesn't actually have a working stove or oven, this explanation seems unlikely.

As the former dwelling place of Utah's celebrated founding father, Forest Farm House would be a spiritual place even if its ghosts never materialized. In it decisions were made about the Mormon Church that allowed it to become a powerful faith with millions of devoted worshipers. Built—like Salt Lake City and Utah—with the blood, sweat and prayers of Brigham Young, the house with the long, round porch is a fitting monument to his memory. Its ghosts serve as colorful reminders of the heroic pioneering age in which he lived.

The Winchester Mystery House
SAN JOSE, CALIFORNIA

Anyone who takes the tour of the famous Winchester House is bound at some point to question the sanity of its architect. There are stairways that lead only to dead ends. There are windows that open into the floor below. Walking blindly through a door can mean falling several feet into another room's sink. The rooms themselves often seem haphazardly built or incomplete, and there are so many of them that a visitor could sleep in a different room each night for half a year before he or she would have to start again. It quickly becomes clear that this house was not built for people to live in.

William Winchester was the son of Oliver Winchester, a clothing manufacturer who had made his fortune by purchasing a struggling rifle company in 1866 and turning it into the most successful business of its kind. Under Oliver's control, the Winchester rifle soon became a ubiquitous sight in America, especially in the Western territories where it was considered foolish to go without one. Wealthy beyond imagining, William could take his pick among the world's debutantes and in the end he chose a lovely young Connecticut woman named Sarah Pardee.

Living a life of uninhibited luxury, the Winchesters spent four blissful years together before Sarah gave birth to a girl they named Annie. At first, Annie appeared to be a plump and healthy child, but as the days went by she began to lose weight. The doctors diagnosed her with marasmus, a disease specific to very young children, and within six months of her birth Annie was laid to rest. The shock forever affected Sarah. Never again would she take pleasure from the extravagant world around her. The presence of death now permeated her life. To make matters worse, just a few months later, William, who had just inherited his father's entire fortune, became ill with tuberculosis. Not long after, he joined his daughter and left Sarah a very rich—but very disturbed—widow.

Concerned that Sarah was drowning in grief, a good friend suggested that she meet with Adam Coons, a spiritualist from Boston who many believed could contact the dead. Hesitant at first, Sarah decided that if seeing him meant at least a few more moments with her lost family, then it would be worth it. Sarah met Adam and within minutes he claimed to be in contact with a man whose description matched William's. Adam began to talk to the ghost, and the conversation soon took a unexpected turn.

"He says your life is in danger," Adam told Sarah. "There are spirits who are angry with your family. Murderously so. He says that they are the ones who are responsible for his and Annie's illnesses."

Shocked and horrified, Sarah spoke up.

"Why? What have we done?"

"He says that they are the ghosts of the people killed by the rifles that bear your name. He says that they are angry because the Winchester rifle has caused them to wander and haunt the earth forever."

"Is there anything I can do? Surely there's something!"

Adam told her that William had an idea.

To ward off ghosts, Sarah Winchester built one of America's most unusual haunted houses.

"Build them a house. Some place where they can stay and end their wanderings. Perhaps then they will forgive you and spare your life."

Afraid for her life, Sarah set about looking for land on which to build the house she believed would save her from the vengeance of the dead. She found a plot on the other side of the country in the Santa Clara Valley, near San Jose, California. When Sarah saw the 162-acre farm with its small, unfinished eight-room farm house, she had a gut instinct that she interpreted as the approval of William. She bought it immediately and ordered a crew of 22 carpenters to work on it day and night. They would do so for the next 36 years.

Sarah believed that each ghost should have a room of its own. No architects were hired to aid in the design; instead, Sarah relied on her instincts, superstitions and dreams. One of the first rooms built, the Blue Room, was where she held séances, during which she got instructions from the ghosts on what to build next. The result was chaos, but deliberate chaos. While she believed that most of the ghosts would be peaceful, she was deathly afraid of those with more malevolent agendas and intentionally designed the house to confuse them. Stairways leading to nowhere were built, as were doors that opened to reveal bare walls. Trapdoors were scattered throughout and many of the bathrooms (only one of which contained a shower) had glass doors, which made privacy impossible. Sarah also insisted on employing the number 13 throughout the house. For example, the windows each had 13 panes of glass and chandeliers that normally held 12 candles were redesigned to hold one more.

After nearly 22 years of construction, the house had over 700 rooms and stood seven stories tall. In a further effort to confuse the negative spirits, Sarah spent each night sleeping in a different room. Despite fears of those spirits who might wish her harm, Sarah grew quite fond of her ethereal guests. A bell tower was constructed and the bell was rung nightly at midnight, 1 AM and 2 AM, so that the good spirits would know that they were welcome to come in and rest. On many occasions, a sumptuous five-course meal was served in the exquisite dining room on 13 solid gold plates—one for Sarah and 12 for any ghosts hungry enough to join her.

One night, however, Sarah believed that the same spirits who had taken her family from her finally found her and did their best to do her in. It was the night of the great San Francisco earthquake—April 18, 1906—that devastated much of California. The fifth, sixth and seventh floors of the house were destroyed and several of the towers toppled over. Sarah survived and had her carpenters redouble their efforts. Although she decided not to rebuild the three decimated floors, construction on the house continued unabated for close to another 20 years.

In the end, only Sarah's death halted the construction. It was rumored that when the house's carpenters were informed of her passing, they stopped immediately, leaving some nails half-hammered into the wood. In keeping with her superstitions, her will was divided into 13 parts and contained 13 signatures. In it, she left almost everything to her niece Francis Marriot, who promptly sold all the mansion's antiques and furnishings and then the mansion itself to a group of investors who wanted to transform Sarah's obsession into a place for tourists to enjoy.

It is ironic that Sarah's house became a popular tourist destination, given the very small number of people who were allowed in it while Sarah was alive. Save herself, some relatives and her servants, very few living guests were ever invited inside the mansion. In fact, at one point Sarah refused to invite in Theodore Roosevelt himself after he had requested a tour of the unique building. The only famous person to ever be allowed into the mansion was the legendary escape artist Harry Houdini, who never talked about what happened during his visit.

Many skeptics question whether Winchester House was ever haunted by ghosts. While several visitors, tourists and staff members have claimed that they witnessed supernatural occurrences inside the house, there is a feeling that the activity has more to do with the house's uniquely spooky design than anything else. Perhaps Sarah Winchester was just a grieving wife and mother who built the house to alleviate a grief she could not vocalize. Then again, in a house that now has 160 rooms, it isn't difficult to believe that somewhere inside a ghost has found a place to rest for a while.

The Golden North Hotel
SKAGWAY, ALASKA

The Golden North Hotel was built in response to the great rush of people who invaded the small Alaska town of Skagway in search of immediate wealth. One of the inevitable results of the gold rush was that for every honest prospector who came into town, there also arrived an equal compliment of thieves, con men, prostitutes and lawyers to unburden him of his little golden treasures. All these people needed places to sleep at night. Although the Golden North was designed to be as classy as possible given the place and time, the hotel's reputation often prevented honest people from staying there. It definitely wasn't an appropriate place for an ambitious young husband to leave his wife by herself, but one of the symptoms of gold

The Golden North Hotel, a haunted remnant of a storied gold rush

fever is an unwillingness to observe common sense, so many husbands did just that. In room 23 the consequences of one such man's decision can still be felt today.

Her name is Mary and she is the Golden North's longest staying guest. Over 100 years have passed since she moved into room 23, and she has no plans to check out. Perhaps only the demolition of the Golden North will force the terrified young ghost to leave her room. Those who have seen her say that she is beautiful, even eternally young, although she occasionally does cough from the illness that killed her.

Mary followed her husband to Alaska. Like many, he dreamed of the instant riches to be found in the mountains and rivers. Knowing that she was too fragile to withstand the harsh unpleasantness of the wilderness life, he got her a room at the Golden North and told her to wait for him. Upon his return, they would never have to worry about money again; this prospect alone made the loneliness of their separation tolerable. Mary very reluctantly agreed, buoyed somewhat by the genuine enthusiasm that bubbled out of him.

While her husband was in the gold fields, Mary became ill. Her lungs filled with fluid and breathing became a painful chore. When the sickness first took hold of her, she wanted to go and see a doctor, but a previous day's incident had left her terrified of leaving her room. She was walking along the outside hallway when she was approached by a large man. Mary tried her best to ignore him, but he had other plans.

"You!" he shouted at her. He was dressed in an expensive suit that looked odd on a man so imposing. His face was scarred and his nose looked liked it had been broken many times. "Stop!" he shouted again.

Mary hurried her pace, but he easily caught up with her and grabbed her roughly by the arm.

"I'm talking to you," he hissed, his open mouth revealing that he was missing a front tooth.

Mary was too scared to say anything.

"Do you know who I am?" he asked.

Mary shook her head.

"I'm the fellow responsible for the protection of the ladies in this area. There's a lot of bad men out there who have no problem doing the most horrible things to a frail thing like yourself. I know 'cause I'm one of them."

Mary stared at him uncomfortably.

"I require payment for my protection. One half of what you earn in a night is what I charge, which by the looks of you is probably a lot."

Mary's face flushed with anger at the man's suggestion that she was a prostitute, but she was still too frightened to correct him.

"So the next time I see you, you better have a wad of bills to hand over. I would hate to see what would happen to you without my protection."

With that final threat he let her go. Mary ran back to her room and locked it shut. From then on she refused to leave her room. Her only outside contact was an employee at the hotel who her husband had paid to keep an eye on her. It was he who brought her food and who eventually got a doctor to come up and examine her when her cough became unbearable. By then it was too late. The pneumonia had taken hold and nothing could be done to cure it. When her husband returned, without the riches he had promised her, Mary was dead. He cursed himself, left Alaska and never dreamed of gold again.

Because Mary had become so afraid of leaving room 23, she remained there even as her spirit left the body that had been unceremoniously disposed of by the authorities. She waits there still. People have seen her looking out of her window, hoping to catch a glimpse of her beloved husband in the street below. Some visitors who have stayed in her room have found it difficult to breathe, as if their lungs have been instantly filled with a heavy syrup. Then, without explanation, the difficulties disappear, leaving guests gasping and wondering what had just happened. Mary's pneumonia may not be contagious, but apparently her despair is.

Skagway's boom quickly waned. Finding more misery than gold, people abandoned the area in droves; within two years of its peak, the town returned to its original population of 800. Although prospectors and opportunists left behind an exhausted wreck of a town, somehow it has managed to transform itself into a quaint remnant of the era that almost destroyed it. The people who live in Skagway today often dress in period costumes and pretend that the town hasn't changed in the last 100 years. But like many who attempt to honor history in this way, the locals feel impelled to whitewash some of the realities of the quaint little town's past. But ghosts such as Mary remember.

4
Wandering Women

Chloe's Mistake
ST. FRANCISVILLE, LOUISIANA

We can thank Margaret Mitchell for the way the word "plantation" swirls around in our heads. Thanks to her novel, *Gone with the Wind* (and the famous film it inspired), the word conjures up images of a large white mansion filled with pretty southern belles and their throngs of suitors. It makes us think of bearded colonels in white suits drinking mint juleps and matronly black women with kerchiefs tied around their heads. To say that this portrait of the past is romanticized is an understatement. Because of slavery, death and misery flourished unabated on southern plantations for many years. They were hotbeds for all the human vices, yielding two kinds of crops—the cotton plants in the fields and the ghosts destined to haunt them.

The Myrtles Plantation in St. Francisville, Louisiana, was built by General David Bradford. Named for the fragrant evergreens that dotted the landscape, the plantation was always a place of incredible pain and cruelty. As a result, it has become home to many different ghosts— every one of which walks the earth in search of justice that can never be served.

The most famous of these ghosts is a woman named Chloe. A mulatto slave born in France, she had been saved from the ravages of the sugarcane fields when she was made a house servant. Her beauty had been spared—an apparent blessing that would prove her undoing.

General Bradford's 14-year-old daughter, Sara Matilda, had married a judge named Clarke Woodruff. By today's

Today, the placid Myrtles Plantation offers little indication of the abuse and racism that was once commonplace.

standards, he would be considered a heartless sociopath, but in his day he was simply considered a slightly temperamental southern gentlemen. Despite his violent tendencies, Judge Woodruff was a highly respected lawyer before he took up the robe, and he counted among his closest friends a future president, Andrew Jackson.

When General Bradford died, Judge Woodruff bought Myrtles from his mother-in-law and moved in with his pregnant wife and their two children. It didn't take long for him to become enamored of the beautiful Chloe. Just hours after she first came to his attention, he had her summoned

to his room. With an animalistic ferocity in his eyes he vio-
lated her. Then he ordered her to come to his room each
night thereafter, so he could do it again and again.

   But among Judge Woodruff's many faults was a fickleness that led him to tire of his unwilling mistress. He soon
chose another house slave to satisfy him. He told Chloe
that if she did anything to displease him, he would have
her sent out to the sugarcane fields, which she feared
more than anything. Chloe tried to get back into his good
graces. To work in the fields meant 18 backbreaking hours
every day in the suffocating heat, with just six hours to
sleep and tend to the small gardens from which the slaves
were expected to feed themselves. To be sent to the fields
was often a death sentence.

   Because of his fickleness and cruelty, Judge Woodruff
was almost impossible to please. Soon Chloe began
eavesdropping on him, hoping to hear something that
would help her in her quest. One day Judge Woodruff
caught her listening in on him. With an insane fury he
dragged her outside and cut off one of her ears in front of
the plantation's other slaves. He told them all that other
eavesdroppers would face a similarly grim punishment.

   Chloe's head was bandaged and she was back at work
the same day. She had never seen the judge so angry and
was terrified that she was going to be sent to the fields.
After the bandages came off, Chloe covered her disfigure-
ment with a green turban. It was then that she hatched a
plan that would have disastrous consequences for everyone involved.

   Chloe picked some white oleander, a southern flower
whose delicate beauty is matched only by the deadliness

of its poison. She hid it away and waited for just the right opportunity.

The birthday of Judge Woodruff's oldest daughter was exactly what she had been waiting for. She asked the cook that she be allowed to bake the cake, and the old woman gratefully agreed. Along with all the customary ingredients, Chloe added a tiny amount of the lethal flower.

At the party, Chloe cut and served the cake. There was a peculiar smile on her face as she gave pieces to Sara and her two daughters. She seemed disappointed when the judge decided to not have any.

When Sara and the two children took ill, Chloe rushed to their aid. She did everything she could, but as the hours passed it became clear that her treatment was having little effect. All three of them complained that they felt numb all over and they were barely able to swallow the tea Chloe made them drink. Then they began to sweat profusely and vomit. They stared out at Chloe with cold accusing eyes. Before the sun set, all three of them were dead.

The clueless Judge Woodruff had no explanation for this sudden tragedy, but the other slaves knew that Chloe was the cause. Afraid that her actions would result in horrible reprisals against everyone, they stormed the house and dragged Chloe out. They gathered around a nearby tree and hanged her from its strongest branch. When they were sure that she was dead they cut down her body, weighted it with stones and threw it into the river. Her body was swept away, but her spirit remained

Over the centuries, Chloe has been spotted many times on the plantation. Once, one of its owners awoke in her

The ghost of a slave named Chloe has often been spotted on the grounds.

bed and saw Chloe standing over her. There was a look of disappointment on the ghost's face, as if she was expecting to find someone else in that bed. Although the owner was frightened by this encounter at first, she found that there was nothing malevolent about Chloe's spirit. Teeta Moss, who bought the mansion in 1992, hadn't realized that Chloe was around when she took some photographs around the grounds. After they were developed, she discovered she had not been alone, as one of the photos featured the ghostly silhouette of Chloe, her green turban visible in the shot.

Chloe is not the only ghost to inhabit the house. The two Woodruff children have also been seen playing around the house. Once, Teeta Moss' young son saw one of the ghost children hanging from a chandelier. Hester Edy, the mansion's curator and tour guide, has claimed that she has twice felt the sensation of an invisible child pulling at her skirt to get her attention. Sometimes they have been seen peeking into windows, and once they frightened a visitor when they appeared suddenly at the foot of his bed.

Not surprisingly, Chloe's hanging did not mark an end to the violence at the plantation. Judge Woodruff himself was later murdered, but apparently he passed peacefully to the other side, as he has never been heard from since. William Winter, on the other hand, chose to stay in the mansion where his murder took place.

A lawyer, William lived at Myrtles with his wife Sarah for 11 years. Leaving one morning for work, he walked out of his house and felt a 100-pound sledge hammer hit him in the chest. Somehow he managed to remain standing as he looked down and saw that he had just been shot. He looked out to identify his assailant but saw no one. Knowing that he had just minutes left, he screamed out his wife's name and managed to make his way back into the house and up to the 17th step of their staircase. Upon hearing her name, Sarah ran down to him and caught him just before he collapsed. He died in her arms. Now his ghost can be heard reenacting this vivid scene over and over again, always stopping on the 17th step.

Other ghosts appear at the Myrtles, but their stories have been lost to history, leaving their presences unexplained. There is, for example, the impish spirit who likes to bounce around on the mansion's beds, rumpling the sheets. This mischief is quickly corrected by the ghost of young woman in a maid's uniform, who follows him from bed to bed, straightening out his mess. Another familiar ghost is that of a Frenchwoman who is forever following the sounds of a crying baby. Going from room to room, she is never able to get to the baby's cries in time. In addition, a piano on the first floor can sometimes be heard at night playing one chord repeatedly, stopping only when someone enters the room to check it out. Once, a dead Confederate soldier was seen and heard on the front porch, and in the gazebo the ghost of a voluptuous Indian woman has been seen lounging comfortably.

But the most chilling reminders of the Myrtles' past are the ghosts of the dead slaves who come by the house, ready to start their chores. Even in death, they are denied the rest they needed so desperately.

Ocean-Born Mary
HENNIKER, NEW HAMPSHIRE

Captain Don Pedro was not a kind man. He was one of the most infamous pirates of his day, and meeting him at sea was as sure a sign of death as any. A firm believer in the phrase "dead men tell no tales," he killed all those he robbed, leaving no evidence of his crimes. He was also a very superstitious man who would rethink his cruel intentions when faced with the possibility that his actions could bring a curse down upon him. It was this side of his personality that spared the lives of the travelers aboard the *Wolf*, an Irish sailing vessel carrying immigrants to New England. It was also how a woman named Mary got her name.

Mary was the daughter of the *Wolf*'s captain, James Wilson. Although she had never set foot on Ireland, the nation's spirit soon become evident in Mary's fiery red hair and in the forthrightness of her nature. She had been born at sea, just a few days before Don Pedro attacked. Her birth proved to be the salvation of the *Wolf* and its passengers.

Correctly identifying the *Wolf* as a passenger ship and therefore easy pickings, Don Pedro and his men attacked and boarded the vessel, intending to leave no one alive. Before the carnage began, Don Pedro heard Mary crying in her mother's arms below deck. He stopped and immediately ordered his men to stand down. To kill adults was one thing, but those who sailed the seas believed that to kill a newborn child resulted in a dangerous curse.

Captain Pedro ordered his men to bring him Captain Wilson, who was prepared to fight to the death for the lives of his wife and daughter. When he was brought before the imposing Spaniard, Wilson became convinced that he had just minutes left to live. He was surprised when the fierce pirate asked him to fetch the child whose cries he had just heard. Captain Wilson hesitated, unsure of Don Pedro's intentions. Although he was afraid of what such a cruel and violent man would do to his first and only child, there was a surprising gentleness in the pirate's voice when he made the request. Captain Wilson took the greatest risk of his life and had his wife and child brought up.

It took one look at the tiny girl for the pirate to lose himself. So moved was he by her porcelain beauty that he spoke to Captain Wilson in a whisper.

"Señor, who is the father of this child?"

Captain Wilson told him that he was the child's father.

"Then I ask you to do me this honor. My mother's name was Maria, and as she is recently dead, I wish to honor her spirit by bestowing her name on another." The large pirate smiled and leaned in close to the captain, adding, "But I am not in a position to be a father." He spoke almost conspiratorially. "So I ask you this—give this child my mother's name and I will spare the lives of everyone on this ship."

Captain Wilson was so relieved that he nearly wept. He immediately accepted Don Pedro's offer, and the child was christened Mary. Don Pedro and his men began to leave the *Wolf*. Just before he reboarded his own ship, he stopped and shouted some words in Spanish to his crew. A minute passed before one of them returned holding a beautiful piece of silk. The crewman gave it to his captain who in turn took it to Captain Wilson.

"Here," the pirate said with a smile. "This is my gift to Maria for her wedding day. Perhaps she will use it for her dress."

With that he left the *Wolf*.

Not long after the Wilsons arrived in New Hampshire, Captain Wilson took ill with a fever and died. He never got a chance to see his daughter blossom into a great beauty, able to have any man she wanted as a husband. In the end she chose Thomas Wallace, a man she had known since she was a child. When they married, she wore a dress fashioned from the silk Don Pedro had given her. Mary had no memories of the pirate, but she enjoyed hearing the story of how the violent pirate had been calmed by her beauty. Secretly she wished someday to meet the man who had spared her family.

Happy together, Mary and Thomas had four sons. Life was good and Mary was content to spend the rest of her days with this man who adored her, but then tragedy struck. The same illness that had claimed her father took hold of Thomas. She stayed by his side, nursing him and tending to his needs as best she could, but the fever proved too strong and Thomas died.

Mary was left a widow with four young sons, little money and almost no opportunities. She struggled as best she could, her fiery Irish heart ensuring the survival of her children. But life was hard and she dreamed of meeting a man who could rescue her from her misery. Then one day, as she chopped wood for a fire, she saw a handsome older man walk along the road in front of her home.

Seeing her, he stopped and walked over to her fence and began to speak.

"Excuse me, Señora," he said with a strong foreign accent, "I am a traveler here. I am in search of a woman I met once many years ago. I once did her a kindness and I hope for her to do me one in return. Her name is Maria, and when I last saw her she was less then a week old. I am told that she lives around here."

Mary stared at the man and knew at once that he was the one who had spared her family and provided her with the material for her wedding dress.

"Don Pedro?"

The Spaniard's face broke into a large smile.

"That is my name, Maria. That is my name."

Mary invited the pirate into her home and learned from him that he had retired and was now in search of a place to rest and grow old. Years of plundering had left him wealthy enough to live anywhere he pleased, but whenever he dreamed of a place to call home he did not see a city or an island. He saw a person. He saw the Irish girl who had captured his heart so long ago, and now that he had found her he asked her to be his wife.

They were married a week later. Mary once again wore the dress made of the silk given to her by her new husband. On their honeymoon night, Don Pedro pledged to be a good father to her sons and to keep his new family from ever again feeling the cold touch of poverty.

With his money Don Pedro bought a huge tract of land and built a beautiful home and a large stable. For the next 10 years he showered Mary with gifts and refused to let her perform even a moment's work. Life to Mary and her sons had become like a dream, which only made the intrusion of reality all the more noticeable.

One night Mary was awakened by the sound of a great weight hitting the earth outside her room. This was followed by the sound of digging. Curious, she got up, put on her robe and went outside to investigate. She edged quietly along the outside of their mansion and stopped when she heard two men whispering out of sight. Mary peeked around the corner and saw her husband and a large man with a long scar along his face place a heavy trunk into a freshly dug hole. Not wanting to disturb them, Mary turned around and went back to her room.

The next day Mary asked Don Pedro about his nocturnal activities. For the first and only time in their marriage, his face turned red with anger and his eyes sparkled with fury.

"You saw nothing!" he shouted at her. "If you wish to stay in this mansion I built for you, you will never speak to anyone about this again!"

Mary did as she was told, although her curiosity tormented her.

Things quickly returned to normal and another year flew by without incident, until one quiet afternoon.

Mary had just returned from a trip into town when she noticed that Don Pedro wasn't in his room napping, as was his custom. She asked a servant where he was and was told that he had left with a visitor. Mary asked who the visitor was and the servant answered that he had never seen the man before, but that he would never forget him as he had a long scar running along his face.

Mary turned pale and ran out of the mansion. She immediately went to where she had seen her husband and the scarred man dig their hole. She found that the ground was undisturbed. She went out to search for her husband and soon found him just a few feet away from their stable. He was dead. A large Spanish sword jutted out of his back. The scarred stranger was nowhere to be found.

Mary had her servants take her husband's body and, following his wishes, place it behind the large hearthstone of the kitchen's fireplace, where it was sealed forever. A widow once again, Mary never remarried.

After his death, the true nature of Don Pedro's identity spread around the state, and soon groups of men in search of pirate gold made their way to Mary's estate. She made no attempt to stop them, as they always kept away from the house and never went near where Mary knew something was buried. The treasure hunters soon gave up, and Mary grew old in the home Don Pedro had built for her. In the 50 years that passed after his death, Mary kept her promise to him and never attempted to find out what was inside that trunk.

Mary died at the age of 94, and her neighbors soon began to claim that they saw her on occasion, walking along the roads, looking as she did when Don Pedro saw her chopping wood that day all those years ago. Some claimed to see her riding in the back of the expensive coach he had bought for her as a wedding gift, but the reports of these visions were easily dismissed as attempts to preserve the memory of a great woman for those who did not know her.

What was seldom discussed was that the people who rented the large mansion after her death never stayed for long. It was accepted among those in the area that perhaps

Mary wanted to keep the house to herself. No one suspected that she was afraid that someone would decide to do some digging along the edge of the house.

Because no one was willing to stay in the mansion, it was abandoned and left in disrepair. For years it stayed that way until it was bought by a Wisconsin woman named Flora Ray and her son Louis. With the help of some workmen, they restored the mansion to its former glory. In order to do some work on its foundation, a trench was dug along one side of the house. To the shock of the excavators, a trunk was found hidden beneath the earth. Their shock turned to disappointment when they opened it and found that it was empty. The trunk was placed in the house's basement and quickly forgotten. It took two years of work for the house to be made livable again, and even when Flora and her son moved in there were still a couple months of cleaning left to do.

The first morning after they moved in, they set about to cleaning out the kitchen, which was full of all sorts of leftovers from the previous tenants. Louis started a fire in the stove and started to burn all the refuse his mother found in the cupboards. He grabbed a paper bag from the pile and was about to throw it in when he felt a firm cold hand grab his wrist and stop him. Louis looked down to where he felt the hand and saw nothing. He turned around and saw only his mother at the other end of the kitchen, too far away to have grabbed him. Louis decided to try again and made another attempt to throw away the bag. Once again he felt the invisible hand around his wrist. He quickly turned around and again saw only his mother, still too far away to have stopped him. Stunned, he opened up the paper bag and nearly had a heart attack when he saw that it contained enough gunpowder to blow up the entire house.

What had changed Mary's mind about sharing the house? Perhaps it was because the Rays had rebuilt the home she loved so much or because they finally eased her mind about the contents of the trunk. Whatever the reason, Mary did all she could to protect Flora and Louis as long as they lived there. After he moved out, Louis claimed that Mary had saved him from potentially fatal injury no less than 16 times. On one memorable occasion, she even helped him save his new car from being crushed in a storm.

A hurricane was sweeping through New England when Louis realized that the small garage he had built himself a few months earlier was swaying precariously in the strong wind. He had built the garage to protect the car he had just bought, and if it went down his car would go with it. So he braved the harsh weather and went outside to try to prop up the garage with some wood he had left over from his initial construction. Louis felt as if he was drowning in an ocean of torrential rain, but he continued until the garage no longer swayed. When he came in, he was as wet and tired as he had ever been in his life. After he got out of his wet clothes, his mother put a warm blanket around his shoulders, sat him in front of the kitchen stove and set about making him a hot cup of tea.

As she began to boil the water, she turned and asked her son a question.

"Who was that helping you out there?"

Louis looked at her with a confused look on his face.

"What do you mean?" he asked her, not sure if he understood the question.

"I saw a woman out there helping you prop up the garage."

"But I was alone," Louis insisted.

"No you weren't. There was a woman helping you out there."

Louis just shrugged his shoulders. It wasn't until Mary began to make appearances in the house that Flora was able to identify the woman she saw that night.

Sure that their house was haunted, Flora and her son invited journalists from all over the country to visit the house and interview them. Their home quickly became famous and Louis was quick to exploit the publicity by charging admission to people who wanted to catch a glimpse of the beautiful specter. Many accused the Rays of being opportunists who had fabricated their stories about Mary in order to make a quick buck.

Their case wasn't helped when sightings of Mary became rarer and rarer. Some took this as proof that she had never existed, while others believed it was simply because she was ready to pass over to the other side. Still others believed that Mary's famous pride would not allow her to become some kind of circus attraction. Whatever the reason, Mary no longer haunts the mansion Don Pedro built for her so many years ago.

The Unsinkable Molly Brown
DENVER, COLORADO

Perhaps the most interesting and telling tidbit about the legendary "Unsinkable Molly Brown" is that she was never actually called Molly while she was alive. The most famous survivor of the *Titanic* sinking was always called Margaret or, in the case of her friends, Maggie. It wasn't until the 1960s, close to 30 years after her death, that she became known as Molly, thanks to *The Unsinkable Molly Brown*, a popular Broadway musical written by Richard Morris and Meredith "The Music Man" Willson (later made into a popular movie starring Debbie Reynolds). It's unclear why the authors changed her name; perhaps Maggie wasn't as musically suitable as Molly or maybe Maggie wasn't quite rustic enough to match the authors' interpretation of the character. Whatever the reason, Margaret Brown's new name has stuck. The Denver museum dedicated to her is called the Molly Brown House and in James Cameron's blockbuster *Titanic,* the famous social climber played by Kathy Bates introduces herself as Molly, not Maggie.

Knowing this information, one cannot help but approach her biography with a hint of skepticism. After all, if her name isn't even historically accurate, how much credence can be placed in the stories and legends that are attributed to her? Even while she was alive, Maggie was happy to let people write stories about her that she knew weren't true. She even aided in the mythmaking by adding her own embellishments. As a result, it is easy to overlook

Margaret "Molly" Brown, socialite and flamboyant Titanic *survivor*

the reports of ghosts at Molly Brown House. But given the number of reports and the passion with which the museum's staff and visitors swear by them, one would be remiss to so casually dismiss them.

Maggie was born in Hannibal, Missouri, in 1867. Among the many falsehoods she perpetuated when she became famous was a childhood friendship between her father, John Tobin, and Hannibal's most famous son,

Samuel Clemens (better known as Mark Twain). The truth was that John was a poor Irish immigrant who found himself in Hannibal around the time that the aspiring writer was first making his mark. It was in Hannibal where John met and married a local woman named Johanna Collins. Both had lost their respective spouses years before. Together they had four more children, Margaret being the second. John worked at the gas works and struggled to support his wife and six children, but eventually he managed to buy a house and to send his girls to grammar school.

Although Maggie's supposed illiteracy is a popular part of her mythos, she could in fact read and write as well as any average person. Maggie finished school at 13 and took a job as a waitress at a local hotel. She would later insist that while she worked there she met Samuel Clemens, who advised her to go search for her fortune out West. Chances are this is another of her exaggerations, but wherever the advice came from, she took it.

In 1886, Maggie traveled with her younger brother Daniel to join their half-sister Mary-Anne and her husband Jack in the small town of Leadville, Colorado. In telling the story of their journey, Maggie claimed that she and her brother traveled by caravan through the West, and that they were robbed along the way by the infamous Jesse James. The truth is they traveled by train. After they arrived, Maggie got a job sewing carpets, draperies and shades in a dry goods store. While there, she met James Joseph Brown, a young miner whose dark good looks made him very popular among Leadville's female residents. Although Maggie did not resemble the pretty blonde Debbie Reynolds who would later portray her in the Hollywood movie, she possessed a strong, inviting personality that made up for her ordinary features. Seeing in her a kindred spirit, J.J. (as James Joseph was better known) proposed to her not long after they met. They married that September and had two children, Lawrence and Catherine, within the next three years.

As a miner, J.J. was liked and respected by his peers. He loved the business and became one of its most innovative and resourceful workers. Relying on his expertise, a group of local investors invited him to join them in a consolidation of several mines and leases. The group named their venture the Ibex Mining Company. J.J. served on the company's board of directors, a job that initially brought little prestige. Silver was trading at its lowest price ever, and the industry was struggling to stay afloat. In 1893, the company made a last-ditch effort at survival by redoubling exploration of the Little Jonny Mine, which had once been a major producer of silver and lead. Constant cave-ins had the other board members ready to give up, but J.J. saved the day by devising a new method to keep the earth steady. Thanks to his efforts, the mine opened and almost immediately struck gold. The vein was so pure and wide that it was considered the world's richest at the time. J.J. and his fellow board members became extremely wealthy men. Maggie was now the wife of a millionaire.

The Browns moved their family into a $30,000 house in Denver. Built out of rusticated lava stone in the Queen Anne style with paneled gables and Romanesque arches, the house perfectly matched Maggie's idea of swank sophistication. They replaced the house's original wooden shingles with more fanciful French tiles and built a large porch at the back, making the house the perfect setting for breaking into Colorado's high society.

Not yet 30, Maggie became obsessed with the trappings of wealth, much to the disdain of her husband. She bought expensive gowns and spent thousands on home decorations and large parties. Although many were enchanted by her style and her wit, some were put off by her lack of pretension and her Catholic upbringing. To improve herself, she traveled extensively and studied the arts and languages. Against J.J.'s wishes, she sent Lawrence and Catherine to boarding schools in Europe, in the hopes of giving them a more sophisticated worldview.

J.J. soon grew tired of his wife's social climbing. Rheumatism and heart problems kept him away from the mines he loved and in 1899 he suffered a paralyzing stroke. He recovered, but the robustness that had made him so attractive as a young man had faded. In 1904 J.J. traveled to Pueblo to relax at a popular spa, and there he met a 22-year-old named Maude. Their dalliance didn't last long, and J.J. was sued for alienation of affection by Maude's husband, Harry D. Call. The lawsuit became the focus of Denver's gossipmongers and humiliated Maggie. The couple spent very little time together after that; five years later, after 23 years of marriage, they separated. In the settlement, Mary kept possession of the house with a $540 cash settlement and a $700 a month allowance. She used the money to travel.

Maggie was in Europe in 1912 when she got the news that her baby grandson, Lawrence, Jr., was ill. When she heard the news, she booked the first available passage to the United States. It was purely by coincidence that the boat she was to travel on, the RMS *Titanic*, was then making its maiden voyage.

Little did Maggie know that she and her fellow passengers would become part of the 20th century's most famous disaster. Upon departure, Maggie's only concern during the journey was finishing a book in which she had become absorbed. She was reading on her bed when a sudden crash shattered her window and threw her to the floor. She got up and watched in amazement as men in their pajamas ran along the gangway. She went back inside her room and stayed there until the noise outside caused her to look out once again. This time she saw an exhausted young man with a horrified expression on his face. He told her to get her life jacket and go to the ship's deck. She did as she was told. Once there, she was informed by other passengers that the ship was sinking. She wasn't terribly frightened by the news. She assumed that even if she couldn't get on a lifeboat she could swim long enough to be rescued. She didn't know that the water was so cold she would die of hypothermia long before anyone would find her. Thankfully, her status as a first-class female passenger ensured that she would not have to find out the hard way.

She found herself in a lifeboat with 13 other women and the ship's quartermaster. Maggie wondered aloud why a lifeboat that could hold many more passengers was put out to sea with so few, but fellow survivors ignored her question. When she later demanded that the quartermaster attempt to rescue passengers who were in the icy water, he angrily rebuffed her, afraid that the panicked passengers would overturn the boat in an effort to come aboard. The lifeboat was adrift for two hours, during which time the quartermaster horrified the 14 women with predictions of days passing without food or water before they were discovered.

He was wrong. They were quickly rescued by the *Carpathia*, whose captain, A.H. Rostrom, would later be awarded a loving cup by Maggie. On board the rescue ship, Maggie used her knowledge of foreign languages to gather information from the immigrant survivors. She also gathered money from her wealthy counterparts, and by the time the *Carpathia* reached New York, $10,000 had been pledged to aid the poorer victims of the disaster. Her efforts made her a national celebrity—the unsinkable Mrs. Brown.

Those in Denver who had once shunned her now welcomed her; Maggie reveled in the limelight. In 1914 she attempted to use her fame to earn a senate seat. Although she failed, she remained active in politics as a member of the National Women's Party. Quick to speak her mind, she was repeatedly sued for a variety of slanderous statements. Until her death in 1932, she remained a vibrant and outspoken public figure, who so delighted in seeing her name in print she didn't care whether or not the story being told was true.

From the time of her separation from J.J. to her death, Maggie spent little time at her house in Denver. Eventually she decided to make some extra money by renting the large building out. The Cosgriff family was the first to live there. They stayed for eight years, from 1911 to 1919. The Keiser family moved in after them and were followed by

Lucille Hubbel, who was evicted for subletting rooms. Maggie then stole Lucille's idea and profited by turning her home into a boardinghouse supervised by her house-keeper, Ella Grable.

By 1932 architectural fashions had changed and the house and its neighborhood fell out of favor. The house was bought in 1933 for $5000, one-sixth of what J.J. had paid for it at the turn of the century. Over the years the house changed hands several times and lost much of its Victorian flair. By the 1960s it was a home for wayward girls and bore little resemblance to the place where the Browns once lived. Thanks, however, to the popularity of the musical and the movie based on Maggie's life, a group of Denver residents decided to restore the house to its early 20th century glory. Today, the house now serves as a museum dedicated to the memory of its most famous resident.

As described by Kerri Atter, the museum's current curator, the house has a palpable energy thanks to the hundreds of men, women and children who have lived and worked in it over the years. While Atter and her staff are quick to attribute the tendency of the house's lights to turn off and on by themselves to faulty wiring, that didn't stop her from inviting two psychics to visit the house. Both came to the same conclusion—that the house was home to not one but many ghosts. One of the first ghosts identified was Maggie's mother, Johanna, who died in the house. In an upstairs bedroom it is common for the lights to flicker and the window's shade to shoot up, revealing Johanna's silhouette to anyone looking outside.

The upstairs may also serve as an afterlife home for Maggie's ex-husband. It was there where the house's previous curator once caught what she thought was a visitor smoking a cigarette. Instead, she found that the smoke had appeared without explanation. Later, according to Atter, she tried to pass off the mysterious smoke as some dust floating in the air, but, as Atter points out, it would take an abnormal amount of dust to be mistaken for a billow of cigarette smoke. Moreover, it is a fact that J.J. was a habitual cigar smoker, and his ghost was one of the several named by the psychics.

Atter also tells the story of a woman who noticed a man in the downstairs mirror while she adjusted her hat. When she turned around, she was amazed to see that no one stood behind her. Yet as she looked back in the mirror, she saw, once again, an angry-looking man in a butler's uniform standing on the stairs.

Another of the house's ghosts was caught on film at a luncheon held by the museum. Right before the guests had begun to arrive, a photographer took a snapshot of the table where all the food was being served. When the picture was developed, he was shocked to see the figure of a woman in Victorian dress standing behind the table. Many believe the photographed phantom is none other than the unsinkable Mrs. Brown.

There is nothing scary or frightening about these ghosts. Atter describes them as helpful and nice, and she believes that they are there to protect the house. Given Maggie's love of publicity, it isn't hard to believe that even in death she would make an effort to help a museum dedicated to her memory.

The legend of Molly Brown is a fascinating mixture of fact and fiction. It is a wonderful example of how the

The ghost of Molly's mother, Johanna, is said to appear in an upstairs bedroom of Molly Brown House.

telling and retelling of a story can change history. Thanks in part to the newspapermen of her time, a stage musical, two movies and her own efforts, Molly's story will not soon be forgotten, even if her real name has.

Lovers in a Dangerous Time
BERNARDSVILLE, NEW JERSEY

Phyllis Parker is a regular visitor at the Bernardsville Public Library in the quiet little town of Bernardsville, New Jersey. She visits so often that the librarians have seen fit to give her a library card, although not once has she ever attempted to check out a book. Given some of the events in Phyllis' life, perhaps her lack of interest in books isn't surprising. After all, she's been dead for 200 years.

Years before the building became a library it served as a private residence; before that it was a tavern. Phyllis lived and worked in this tavern with her father, Captain John Parker. She was a striking young lady with coal-black hair, and many of the men in Bernardsville enjoyed visiting the tavern just to hear her laugh and watch as she served food and large mugs of beer. One of these men was the local doctor, a charming man with a swarthy complexion who went by the name of Byram.

Of all Phyllis' potential suitors, he was the one who had what it took to win Phyllis over. Not long after their first meeting they became engaged to be married. So enamored was Phyllis of her charismatic doctor that she overlooked some major inconsistencies in his background. For starters, he never seemed to practice medicine. Worse, he was often away for long unexplained stretches of time. When her father alerted her to this odd behavior, Phyllis dismissed him outright.

"I know for certain he loves me, and for as long as he does I could care less if he was the Devil himself."

The couple's romance blossomed at the outset of the American Revolutionary War. The colonies were demanding to be free from the tyranny of a king who did not have their best interests at heart. Captain Parker's tavern was soon a popular destination for American soldiers who wanted to relax and spend the night. One of these men was an American general named Anthony White. A tall, imposing man who instilled in his men a sense of loyalty few could match, General White was often assigned very important and dangerous missions, as he was one of the few soldiers who could always guarantee success.

Arriving at the tavern with a small garrison of men, the general carried a pouch with him containing several strategic documents. It was vitally important to the colonies that these documents not fall into the hands of the British, since it could mean the deaths of thousands of revolutionaries. Despite their importance, the general left them unguarded in his room. He had been to this tavern many times before in the course of his journeys and had never met anyone there who might steal them. This oversight proved to be costly. When he returned to his room, he found, to his horror, that the pouch and the documents it carried had been stolen. He grabbed his musket and ran to the serving room, which was buzzing with the sounds of genial reveling.

"Quiet!" the general ordered, his voice so strong and passionate that everyone immediately did as they were told. "No one leaves here until the documents that were stolen from my room are returned to me."

Unfortunately, it soon became clear that each person inside had an alibi proving him or her innocent. White asked Captain Parker if he knew of anyone who he had seen in the tavern who might have taken the documents. The captain hesitated. He had an answer for the general, but he was afraid that giving it could mean disaster for the man his daughter loved. His loyalty to the cause, however, emerged victorious and he spoke up.

"There is a man whose comings and goings have always struck me as odd. He claims to be a doctor and he goes by the name of Byram. I know for certain that he was in here today."

"Describe him to me," the general insisted.

"He is a tall man, much like yourself. His clothes are fine and his boots are always polished. His skin is like that of a man from Greece or Italy, but I believe he was born in London." The captain went on to describe Dr. Byram in even greater detail. As he spoke, the general created a mental image of the man in his head and soon came to an important conclusion.

"Thank you, Captain. If I am right, the man you have just described to me is Aaron Wilde. He is a British spy and we have been searching for him for some time. Where does he live?"

The captain told him and the general gathered his men.

Dr. Byram was asleep when the soldiers broke into the room he was staying in.

"What the blazes!" he swore as he was awakened by the noise. He sat up in his bed and watched as General White walked in through his door.

"So it is you, Mr. Wilde. You managed to escape from us the last time we caught you, but today I'm afraid you will not be so lucky."

The soldiers ransacked the room and quickly found the stolen documents hidden beneath a loose floorboard. The spy knew his number was up and he did not struggle when the men arrested him. General White and his soldiers marched with their prisoner to the end of town, where a makeshift gallows had been arranged. Not wanting him to escape from their grasp again, they immediately put the noose around his neck and asked him if he had anything he wanted to say.

"Just tell her that I am sorry."

The box he stood on was kicked out from under him; it took several minutes before his body stopped twitching.

The general was content to leave the spy's body to hang and rot as a reminder to all those who might imitate his treachery, but Captain Parker decided to protect his daughter from the truth and had the body cut down and sealed in a wooden casket.

Phyllis was shocked when she saw a group of men bring a casket into the tavern. She asked her father what was happening. Unable to tell her the whole truth, he simply told her that the wooden box contained a hanged traitor and that the body would buried in the morning. Phyllis did not question her father, but her imagination started to run rampant.

That night Phyllis had a dream. In it she saw her fiancé trying to claw his way out of a very small enclosed space. His fingers were raw and bloody and he was beginning to suffocate.

"Save me, Phyllis!" he screamed with his last breath.

His scream frightened her awake. Almost as if possessed, she ran out of her room, found an ax and ran to the casket that still sat in the tavern. She brought the ax down on it over and over again, as if she knew what she would discover. Finally she saw the man who lay inside and she screamed and screamed. She never recovered from her discovery. As the years went by, she sank deeper into hopeless insanity.

Not even her death would ease her suffering. After she died, there were strong hints that her spirit had not left the house. A hundred years passed before it became clear that not only was she still there, but that her pain had worsened.

By then the building had been turned into a house with a young family occupying it. With her husband away on business, the young mother had just put her baby to sleep. She was sitting down to do some sewing when she heard what sounded like a group of men carrying something heavy. Frightened by the possibility of a burglary, she stayed in her room, afraid that she might be killed if she confronted the intruders. She next heard the sound of a large object hitting the floor with a loud thud. The men left and she sat there in silence, waiting for them to return.

What she heard next was not the sound of a group of men, but instead the loud bangs of an ax ferociously chopping wood. The violent noise awoke the baby, who began to cry. Fearing for her child, the young mother ran from her room to her baby, locking the bedroom door behind her. She held her child close to her and tried to calm it, although she herself was close to tears. Then there arose a scream of such terror and heartbreak it would haunt her for the rest of her days.

The scream ebbed into a wail of grief that eventually faded to silence. Hours later, the young mother felt safe enough to leave the room and investigate. What she found was an empty house that was in every way undisturbed. There was no evidence that anyone other than herself and her baby had been inside. When her husband returned the next day, the young mother told him of the bizarre occurrence and of the terror she had felt. She told him about the strange noises and the horrible heart-rending scream that she claimed she could still feel in her bones.

At first the young man dismissed his wife's story as a product of her overactive imagination, but a year later he was told a story that turned his face pale. A friend of his who was interested in local history told him how Phyllis had discovered her fiancé's corpse that tragic night. The young father knew then what his wife had heard the night he was away. Not long after his discovery, he decided to sell the house and move his family to a much less historic location.

Many more encounters with Phyllis were recorded in the intervening years, most often involving the sounds of footsteps, the swish of an old dress or doors and windows opening and closing. When the building became a library, many of the librarians claimed to hear or see something they could not explain. One staff member, Maria Mandala, heard the sound of a woman singing, although she knew she was the only person inside. Martha Hamill, another librarian, heard what she described as the sound of children whispering and sharing secrets. There have also been two incidents in which the phantom Phyllis actually made herself visible. On one occasion, she materialized before a rookie police officer named John Maddaluna, who at first thought she was an intruder until she vanished inexplicably. The other time, Phyllis' spirit appeared before a young boy who said hello to her but did not receive a greeting in return.

Over the centuries Phyllis' pain has not diminished, and she still haunts the place where she discovered her lover's corpse. It is no wonder, then, that her library card goes unused, and that she takes no time to read the books that surround her. Perhaps she feels unable to read others' stories until her own comes to a long-overdue end.

Hidden Away
NARRAGANSETT, RHODE ISLAND

The Squire children saw her first. Dressed in black with a veil over her face and a comb in her hair, she stood by the large mansion's third-floor windows and looked out to the sea and wept. As the years passed, others who came to live in the house saw her as well, always staring and pointing out to sea. Tears streamed down her cheeks like a child who had forever lost her family.

The mansion—all four stories of it—had been built by Japhet Wedderburn, a rich sea captain who called the Rhode Island city of Narragansett his home. Although the exterior of the house was impressive, with green shutters and a large ornate door, its interior was much more spartan, with large rooms and a gallery on the third floor whose windows offered an impressive view of the sea. Captain Wedderburn, who made his fortune trading with the Chinese, was little concerned with the interior because he was usually away at sea for stretches that lasted for months and even years on end. His home was watched over by his housekeeper, Huldy Craddock, who believed the captain needed a woman with whom he could share his company. So it came as no surprise to her when one day he returned from a trip with a strange and beautiful lady on his arm.

She was a tiny waif-like woman. She wore a black dress with a veil; a high tortoiseshell comb held back her thick black hair. She was Dona Mercedes, a wealthy Spanish woman Captain Wedderburn had met in Barbados and married soon thereafter. She did not speak a word of English, but she seemed happy to spend time with her new husband, who took great pleasure in her charm and beauty. Soon, though, the captain was forced to return to sea, leaving the lovely señora with only Huldy for companionship.

Not long after the captain left, a package arrived for Dona from her family. Overjoyed, she opened it and read and reread the letters from her parents and her brothers and sisters. The words in these letters brought tears to Dona's eyes and awakened a profound longing to return to her home in the Caribbean. In the days that followed, Huldy would find Dona pacing in front of the large gallery windows on the third floor, weeping and pointing out to the sea, wanting to go back home to her friends and her family. Huldy tried to ease her despair by taking her into the city to shop and by teaching her how to speak English, but Dona soon refused to leave the large house and often went without food in protest to what she had felt had become an imprisonment.

Slowly the months passed and finally the captain returned. He was shocked to find that his wife now seemed to hate him and his house; she screamed at him to take her back to her home and her loved ones. Captain Wedderburn couldn't understand why Dona was so upset. He had left her in a beautiful house in a beautiful city where an exotic young woman should have had no trouble making friends once she had learned the language. But the more he tried to calm her, the shriller she became, nagging him incessantly in Spanish to take her back to where he had found her.

As their arguments raged, Huldy took ill with a stomach malady and was forced to leave the mansion to rest at her sister's place. When it became clear that she wouldn't return before the captain would set sail again, her sister asked the judge if she should find him a new servant to look after the house and Mrs. Wedderburn.

"No," the captain told her, his voice full of anger and irritation. "Mrs. Wedderburn is accompanying me. I'm taking her back to Barbados so she can visit her family."

For two years, Wedderburn Mansion sat empty until the captain finally returned. Alone.

He explained that his wife had decided to stay on a bit longer with her parents and that all involved thought it was for the best. Soon thereafter he returned to sea where he took ill and died before he could return home to Narragansett.

His large home was sold to a family of five. The Squires loved the spacious rooms, which provided them ample room to entertain guests and live in comfort. They especially enjoyed the third-floor gallery and the magnificent view it afforded. It was the children who first saw the young woman standing in front of those windows, weeping and pointing out into the distance. Yet when any attempt to approach her was made, she vanished.

Later, after the Squires sold the house, other tenants also saw the young woman and noted the sorrow on her face as she tearfully whispered in a foreign tongue. Although the identity of the spirit was no mystery, why she chose to stay and haunt the home that she hated so thoroughly in life remained unclear for 50 years—until a shocking discovery was made.

The house was bought by a charitable organization to serve as a summer retreat for Narragansett's poorer children. Workmen descended on it to make all the necessary renovations. They found the fireplace in such a poor state that it had to be removed and replaced. What they found when the wall behind the hearth was cracked open explained the tears of the mansion's phantom.

Inside a deep hole sat a makeshift wooden coffin that contained the wrapped remains of a small woman. The skeleton wore a black dress and had a tortoiseshell comb in its hair.

Dona Mercedes Wedderburn never did return to Barbados. But she can still be found on occasion standing in front of those large windows, dreaming of a time when she will be able to return to the loved ones she has missed these many years.

She Earned It
NEW YORK, NEW YORK

Unlike ghosts who linger among the living out of revenge or despair, Eliza Jumel seems to stick around out of spite. A cold, calculating woman while alive, she does not haunt the Morris–Jumel Mansion in New York City as a reminder of a past injustice (most of the house's injustices were actually her gleeful work), but rather because she refuses to leave a house that she so ruthlessly made her own.

Born into extreme poverty, Eliza became a prostitute at a young age in order to support herself. She was so hardened by the cruelties of life that she jumped at the first chance to escape. She met Stephen Jumel, a wealthy businessman, and soon convinced him to make her his wife. Yet in spite of her newfound wealth, she found that her husband's peers refused to accept her, so she traveled with Stephen to France where she became an ardent supporter of Napoleon Bonaparte. When he was exiled, she left her husband behind in France and returned to New York where she sold Stephen's business holdings behind his back. She kept all the profits and soon turned her husband into a pauper. She used the money to buy herself the acceptance she craved, and once she had it she rid herself of the husband she no longer needed.

One day, Stephen was accidentally stabbed by a pitchfork. A doctor bandaged the distraught man, but Eliza later pulled off his bandages, causing Stephen to bleed to death while he was asleep. A year later, she tried to court even more favor by marrying former vice-president

The Morris–Jumel Mansion, circa 1936

Aaron Burr, who cheated on her and misused her money in much the same way she had with her first husband. He died on the day they were divorced; she lived for another 30 years. Perhaps fittingly, she lost the social acceptance she had fought so hard to achieve. The one thing, though, that could never be taken away from her was her home—a great mansion in Harlem, which today stands as the oldest private residence in Manhattan.

Nearly 70 years after she died, Eliza made her first major appearance as a ghost. A large group of schoolchildren had gathered outside the mansion to take its famous tour. From the third-floor balcony Eliza told them to be quiet. Ever since, the balcony has been her spot of preference, from which she is always ready to scold anybody rude enough to be noisy outside her house.

It should come as no surprise that a house with such an unpleasant former proprietor has more than one ghost. One unnamed apparition, dressed in the uniform of a colonial-era soldier, frightened one man so badly that he dropped dead of a heart attack where he stood. While the identity of that ghost has yet to be determined, it is a fact that the mansion once served as George Washington's base of operations in New York.

The spirit of Eliza's murdered first husband, Stephen, has also made his presence felt in the mansion's halls. His specter was full of so much anger and despair that a group of mediums took pity on him and held two rescue séances that allowed him to successfully pass over to the other side.

Finally, there is the young woman who haunts the servants' quarters. A pretty waif of a girl, she fell in love with one of the Jumels' relatives, who used her love to take advantage of her. When she realized that her lover had no intention of ever marrying her, she jumped from the mansion's roof to her death. As her ghost moves along the mansion's top floor, she can be heard weeping and wailing for the man who so cravenly used her.

Ghosts are almost inevitable at the Morris–Jumel Mansion. Someone as ruthless and determined as Eliza Jumel could never be expected to leave the house for which she would stop at nothing to keep. Unlike the building's other ghosts, who have cause to stay behind, Eliza is bound to the property by her insatiable greed. Perhaps, like Stephen, the other ghosts can be rescued and sent to the other side, but one suspects that Eliza will remain there as long as the mansion stands. She earned it.

The Lady in Black
BOSTON, MASSACHUSETTS

Union guards at Boston's Fort Warren had more to be wary of than the Confederate prisoners under their supervision. A ghost called the Lady in Black had reason to wreak vengeance on those who served the North, and whenever the opportunity arose she would seize it. One sentry, alone at his station late at night, felt slender and delicate hands wrap themselves around his throat, and as he turned away they did their best to choke the life out of him. When he saw the ghost, bathed in a mysterious light, she vanished suddenly and he dropped to the ground gasping for air.

Located on Georges Island in Boston Harbor, Fort Warren was first intended to serve as a defense from sea attack, but by the time it was completed the nation was embroiled in the Civil War. The federal government turned the fort into a military prison where many Confederate prisoners of war were sent after being captured. It was garrisoned until the end of World War I, and then for the decade that followed was downgraded to caretaker status. After the bombing of Pearl Harbor, it was regarrisoned and remained so until 1950 when it was finally closed down for good. During the fort's long history, there was only one thing more terrifying than enemy attack—and she was certainly something to behold.

Melanie Lanier was the beautiful young wife of Lieutenant Andrew Lanier, a Confederate soldier who was captured by Union forces, along with some 600 others during the Civil War. A brave woman, hardened by the war and willing to sacrifice anything for the cause, Melanie made it her mission to free her husband from the prison he had been left to rot in. With what was left of her husband's fortune Melanie made her way through the war-torn country. Her journey took her from her home in Texas to just a few miles away from the island in Boston Harbor where Andrew was imprisoned. By making it this far, she had proved herself much braver than many of the men she set out to rescue.

With her last remaining dollars Melanie bought a small boat. Dressed in a man's suit with her long black hair covered by a hat, she rowed herself to the island on which Fort Warren sat. She managed to make it ashore without being seen. Carrying a shovel, a pickax and a pistol, she was helped by the dark suit, which allowed her to disappear in the shadows and stealthily sneak past the Union soldiers who stood at guard. After an hour of searching, she found her husband and his men. Together they set about digging a tunnel big enough for them all to escape through. They would deal with the water surrounding the island when they came to it.

Fueled by hunger and desperation, the haggard crew worked all through the night. They were mere feet away from escape when they were discovered by a group of armed Union soldiers, who drew their weapons and ordered them to desist. The men surrendered, but Melanie, who had come too far to stop now, drew her pistol and aimed it at the colonel in charge. Her husband, fearing they were going to kill her, shouted at her to drop the gun, but instead she pulled the trigger.

The gun was damp from the rain and it misfired. The colonel's life was spared, but Melanie's husband's was not. A fragment from the bullet entered his skull, killing him before his body hit the ground. Too shocked to cry or speak, Melanie was captured, along with the other attempted escapees. Soon enough, she was sentenced to be hanged.

Moved perhaps by her resolve and beauty, the Union soldiers asked the doomed young woman if she had a last request. Since she was still dressed in the dark men's suit she wore as a disguise, she asked them if they could find her a dress to wear at the gallows. They searched around and found a dark monk's robe in a trunk left behind by a traveling theater company.

On the day of her execution, Melanie put the robe on and waited. When they came to get her, she walked quietly to the gallows. As she stood on the platform she began to whisper under her breath. Her executioner assumed she was praying—which he had seen many times before—but she was not. She was vowing revenge. The noose slipped around her neck and the platform dropped open. The yank of the rope broke her neck and killed her instantly, but it soon became clear that Melanie could not be disposed of so easily.

Within a fortnight of her burial, strange signs began to appear around the fort. In addition to hearing footsteps coming from the shadows, soldiers reported sudden chills that took hold of them when the footsteps stopped. There was also the constant paranoid feeling that someone somewhere was watching them. The soldiers began to speculate about who or what was causing the phenomena, but it wasn't until a young soldier was nearly strangled to death that they realized Melanie Lanier had managed to keep her vow of revenge. Because she appeared in the monk's robe, the men called her apparition the Lady in Black. She lived in the fort's shadows. Concealed by the darkness, she waited for the moments when she could best attack. Her anger consumed her; it demanded retribution, and she spared no opportunity to satisfy her wrath.

A Confederate to the last, Melanie did not leave the fort when the war ended. The South may have surrendered, but she would not. In her mind, every soldier, regardless of where he was from, was now a Union soldier and was to blame for the shot that killed her husband and the noose that broke her neck.

The years passed. When the U.S. entered World War II, the fort found itself regarrisoned. Serving there was a soldier who bore a small resemblance to the Union colonel whose life was spared through the misfortune of Melanie's husband. Whether she thought him the same man or a possible relation, Melanie chose to make his life a living hell. Like the man she nearly succeeded in asphyxiating, this unfortunate boy was left alone at night to guard his station. Warned about the vengeful lady in the shadows, he laughed her off, convinced that it was just a story told

to frighten the newcomers, many of whom were often literally just off the farm.

After several long and boring hours, the young man
heard the sound of footsteps in the shadows. He drew his
rifle and shouted into the darkness.

"Identify yourself!" Somehow he managed to avoid
sounding as scared as he felt.

The footsteps continued. They moved closer and
closer towards them, but all the young sentinel could see
was the pervasive blackness of the shadows.

"I said identify yourself!" he shouted again. "Don't
make me shoot you!"

The footsteps drew even closer, and this time the
young man could see the glint off someone's eye in the
darkness.

"This is your last warning! Identify yourself or I will
shoot!"

From out of the shadows there stepped out a beautiful
woman dressed in a long black robe. The young guard was
so shocked by her appearance that he accidentally pulled
the trigger of his rifle. The bullet discharged and hit the
woman at point blank range—or at least it should have.
Instead, the bullet passed through her as if she wasn't
there.

The young soldier started to scream, but the Lady in
Black simply put her finger to her lips and the sound died
in his throat. Incapable of speaking, he stared at her in
disbelief. Her hair was long and wild and as dark as a
raven's feather. Her skin was pale, as if she had not seen
the sun for decades, and her lips were wide and red; they
smiled at him in a way he did not find comforting.

"At last I have found you." Her voice was calm and bore traces of a delicate southern lilt. Her lips never moved. "Do you have any idea how long I have waited for you?"

He shook his head.

"A very long time. Do you know the agony I felt when the bullet that was meant for you killed my Andrew?"

The soldier tried to tell her that he had never seen her before and that he had no idea who Andrew was or why any bullets were fired in the first place, but he could not speak.

The Lady in Black raised her hands and grabbed the young soldier's head. She leaned in close and whispered in his ear.

"This is what it felt like."

Something happened then. The young soldier spent 20 years in an insane asylum trying to explain it, but his descriptions never made much sense. Madness overtook him and he babbled and wept until the day he died, filled with the memories of a ghost from the most bitter and costly war in American history.

Fort Warren is a historic park now. Boston school-children visit it on field trips for their history classes. The Lady in Black has not been seen there for some time. Perhaps the absence of soldiers leaves her without victims or maybe she believes that the young soldier she terrified so completely was the man she had been searching for all along. Either way, one hopes she has been reunited with the husband she so bravely attempted to rescue.

5

Haunted History

Peter and Fannie
CHAPEL HILL, NORTH CAROLINA

Peter Dromgoole was exactly the type of bad boy many women find irresistible. A hard-drinking, fast-riding gambler, he was the scion of a prominent Virginia family who had sent him to the University of North Carolina in the hopes that news of his rowdy behavior would not travel back to them. During his brief tenure at UNC, little, if any, of his time was reserved for books, especially since there were horses to race and women to seduce. Peter seemed to have no patience for any of the rules and conventions that governed life on campus, and it was clear to all those around him that unless fate intervened he would not live long enough to graduate.

Fannie (whose surname has not survived the retellings of this story) was considered the most beautiful woman in Chapel Hill. A small woman with a delicate frame and frail temperament, she was possessed of that uniquely feminine quality that bewitched men and inspired them to shield her from the dangers of the world. When Peter met her, he had a character-shattering epiphany. From that moment on, he resolved to correct his every flaw so that she would feel the same for him as he for her. He stopped drinking and gave up gambling. He rode his horses at a sensible gallop and he took to his books so that he could amuse his love with his learning. His metamorphosis proved successful. Despite the swarms of suitors that buzzed and flitted about Fannie, she fell for the handsome young man who played the boring stiff, but whose eyes betrayed a sense of rebellion she found intoxicating.

Needless to say, the rejected suitors were resentful. One of them, another student whose name has been lost to time, loved Fannie every bit as much as Peter did, and seeing her in the arms of another drove him to the brink of madness. Fully aware of Peter's reputation as a libertine, he was sure that if he allowed the two to stay together it would mean the ruination of Fannie's reputation—a prospect he refused to consider.

As spring turned to summer, the rejected suitor saw no other solution. He confronted Peter on the campus grounds and told him in no uncertain terms that he would not allow him to despoil the young woman he loved. Peter responded by laughing in the man's face.

"Who are you to say this to me? I love Fannie and she loves me. I fail to see how that is any business of yours."

"It is my business because I know that a man such as you is incapable of love. You are using her, sir! I will not allow that to happen!"

"And how do you intend to back up your threat?" Peter demanded.

His antagonist stiffened noticeably. He had hoped it would not come to this, but he was prepared to go all the way.

"Pistols at dawn," he hissed under his breath.

Peter was so enraged by his accuser's impertinence that he failed to consider the consequences of his response.

"Very well. Where shall we meet?"

"Piney Prospect. Up on the hill."

Both men arranged for friends of theirs to serve as seconds. They all arrived at Piney Prospect as the sun rose in the morning sky.

Peter, having considered the foolishness of their situation, gave his opponent a chance to bow out without any loss of honor.

"Are you a coward, Peter?" was the response that sealed both men's fates.

The pistols were loaded, each with one bullet, and the duelists were placed back to back. At the command of their seconds, they began to walk ten paces forward before they turned, faced each other and fired their guns. Peter's aim was off and he missed his mark completely. His rival fared better. His bullet tore a hole in Peter's chest. His legs gave out from under him and he collapsed onto a flat rock. As Peter bled to death, the three witnesses were instantly sobered by the gravity of their wicked game.

Panicked, they saw no other solution than to bury him as soon as possible. They dug a shallow grave right next to the rock on which his body lay. When they lifted him off of the rock they found that it had been stained dark red by his blood. Too frightened to worry about the blood, they laid his corpse in their hastily prepared grave and swore to each other that they would never speak of the duel again. All three men not only left the university, they all left the state as well.

The days turned into weeks and rumors began to spread about the cause of Peter's disappearance. Before he had met Fannie, he often exclaimed that he would escape from all this pointless study and join the army. Almost everyone assumed that this was what he had done.

But Fannie was incredulous, since she had been privileged enough to see the sincerity that her lover had hidden so well. She knew he would never leave her, and if for some reason he ever had to, he would never leave without going to her first.

One night, months after Peter had last been seen, Fannie awoke from her bed with a start. As if possessed, she ran to Piney Prospect wearing nothing but her nightgown. Shivering in the cold, she found herself standing above a rock whose face was discolored by an unnatural red. She lay down on the rock, closed her eyes and knew everything. She knew why the rock was red and why Peter had been gone for so long.

When her worried family found her, the effects of the cold had already started to take hold. They tried to nurse her back to health, but it soon became clear that Fannie did not want to get better.

"He's so alone," Fannie whispered one night, as gentle tears fell from her much-admired blue eyes. "He's waiting for me. I have to go see him."

Hours later, Fannie was dead.

Not long after her body was laid to rest, people began to see the two lovers together at Piney Prospect. They were always spotted by the rock where Fannie had been found on that bitterly cold night. No one ever suspected that the place was where Peter's fate had also been sealed. Sixty years would pass before his murderer, having carried the burden of his guilt for so many years, confessed to his actions on his deathbed.

It is ironic that the murderer ensured that Peter and Fannie would be together for eternity. If he had not taken action, Peter's infatuation might have waned and he might have made good on his promise to leave for more exciting adventures. Perhaps Fannie would have become available. Instead, Peter's rival made certain that their love would stand for longer than time could record.

The red-stained rock that served as Peter and Fannie's altar can still be found at Piney Prospect. The two lovers are often seen there holding hands and whispering words of adoration to each other. As tragic as their tale proved to be, there is some relief in the notion that even their deaths proved trivial in comparison to their great passion. If, as some claim, love does indeed conquer all, then there are few examples as sublime as the two young spirits who haunt Chapel Hill.

Fort Delaware
DELAWARE CITY, DELAWARE

It was the cold that caused so much misery. The Confederate soldiers imprisoned at Fort Delaware, a large fort on a small Delaware River island just a mile from Delaware City, were southerners unaccustomed to the bitter cold of winter. Always dangerously overcrowded, the fort was almost bearable during the summer (if the inmates could get used to the mud and the rank smell of marsh water), but during the long winter, life became a torture almost impossible to endure.

Over the course of the Civil War, 30,000 Confederate prisoners were detained at the fort. At maximum capacity, in 1863, the fort held 12,500 men. It had been built to

Fort Delaware served as a Confederate prison during the Civil War.

hold 2000, but as more and more Confederates surrendered, the order came from Washington to find room, even if it did not exist. Thanks to this reckless overcrowding, 3000 men died before they could be released. Many people believe that the ghosts of these men haunt the fort, which now stands as a historical monument to the past.

According to legend, Pea Patch Island got its name when a pre-revolutionary boat carrying a shipment of peas crashed into it and caused the green vegetable to sprout all over its beach. At the time, the island was an unappealing 70 acres of sand and mud, with few trees and no animal life. Throughout the years, attempts were made to build on the island, but none of these projects was ever completed. In 1847, the federal government decided that Pea Patch was the ideal location for a citadel that would protect the waterways that lead to Philadelphia. One million dollars was allocated for the construction, but by 1848 the cost of building the fort's foundation on the soft, wet ground ate up the budget. Feeling that the fort was of vital importance, the government raised another million dollars, which allowed construction proper to begin. Designed to be the largest fort in the country, it took over a decade to complete. By 1859, it was garrisoned and the government only had to wait two years to find out that the fort was a wise investment.

The pentagonal fort's solid granite walls were 32 feet high and varied from 7 to 30 feet thick. It was surrounded by a moat 30 feet wide and was only accessible through a drawbridge on its southwest side. Fort Delaware covered six acres of land, but by the time the Confederate prisoners began to arrive, it became evident that many of them would have to be kept outside the fort.

Although the fort was never intended to be a prison, barracks were built inside it when the government decided it was the perfect place to hold captives after the battle of Kernstown in 1862. The wooden shacks were hastily built and offered little more than basic shelter from wind or rain. Inside the fort, there was room enough for only 2000 prisoners, but when that capacity was met the order came from Washington to make room for more. More shacks and some tents were built around the fort on the island, and most of the prisoners ended up staying in them.

To isolate themselves from the reality of their situation, the prisoners did their best to become a mini-community in which as many of the activities of civilian life could be recreated. The men held concerts and plays, staged debates and set up charitable organizations to help the less fortunate among them. They wrote a newspaper, each copy of which was laboriously hand-written, and included advertisements for the various tradesmen and merchants who had set up businesses in the camp. These businesses allowed the money that had been sneaked into the camp to circulate among the prisoners who used it to buy better food and supplies and to gamble.

As diverting as these activities were, they did little to take away the misery that overtook the camp when winter came. With only one wood-burning stove for every 200 men (each of whom had been supplied with only a thin overcoat and a single blanket to combat the cold), the prisoners spent a lot of time positioning themselves close enough to the heat so they could feel its warmth. Some men were so obsessed with keeping warm that they were called Stove Rats and had to be moved forcibly so that others could get close to the heat. The results of these highly organized removal efforts were usually bloody, and it wasn't uncommon for a removed Stove Rat to swear revenge against the men who took his spot.

Revenge, however, was hard to come by, since many of the men were overcome with smallpox, measles, dysentery, scurvy and a host of other diseases. Little could be done to treat these men, as medical supplies were virtually nonexistent. The best an ailing prisoner could hope for

Many inmates succumbed to cold, disease or overcrowding; some have returned as ghosts.

were a few placebos and a mysterious white powder that many assumed was probably just sifted flour.

Given the suffering that the prisoners were forced to accept as part of their daily life, it isn't any surprise that many of them tried to escape. In order to cross the Delaware River, some prisoners attempted to fashion rafts out of anything they could find, while others tried to swim their way to freedom. The possibility of drowning wasn't the only concern these men faced. Patrol boats frequently sailed around the island, and the river was rumored to contain its fair share of sharks.

Those unwilling to take these risks resorted to more creative methods of escape. Some, knowing that the dead were sent to the cemetery at Finn's Point, New Jersey, across the river adjoining nearby Fort Mott, hid themselves in coffins. While some were fortunate enough to make their way into an empty casket, most who attempted this stunt were forced to share their journey with the dead bodies of men who smelled horribly unpleasant when they were still alive. The problem with this method of escape was that a prisoner always ran the risk of passing out after being overcome by the stench of his coffin mate. An unlucky prisoner could easily find himself buried alive face first with a rotting corpse—a situation which made the coldest winter night at the camp seem like a happy holiday.

Other escapees were able to find their way off the island by killing a Union guard and assuming his identity. With the large number of people coming and going from the island, this proposition was safer, although a slipped accent or unlucky coincidence could easily result in the escapee being shot. The safest and easiest way for a prisoner to escape was to bribe the guards, but for many the amount of money required for this maneuver was too much to even contemplate. In the end, the fort's official records indicated that 273 men managed to escape from the fort. How many of them managed to survive and make it to freedom is unknown.

With these facts in mind, it seems a small miracle that the fort's death count of around 3000 wasn't much higher. Ninety percent of the men who found themselves detained at the camp were able to leave alive. Many of them would later attribute their survival to the spiritual awakening they experienced when confronted by the horrors of their situation. The men who were not already religious found themselves turning to prayer to get them through the day. Religious services and Bible classes were held, and in 1863 the prisoners built a chapel. Sadly, they were not allowed to use it because mass gatherings were forbidden by the fort's commanding officers.

After the war ended, the number of soldiers at Fort Delaware fluctuated greatly with the times. It went from almost completely empty in 1903 to fully garrisoned during World War I. Finally, in 1944, the fort was declared surplus property by the federal government. Five years later, it was turned over to the Delaware state government, which in turn turned it into a historical preservation site. Since then it has become a popular Delaware tourist attraction, and it is thanks to these visitors that stories of ghosts on the island have started to surface.

The most common story concerns the appearance of ghostly Confederate soldiers on the island. These translucent spirits have been seen both inside and outside the fort. Dressed in clothes torn and worn with age, these psychic remnants of rebel prisoners are seen shivering and chattering, no matter what the weather. Their skin is tinged blue and bears the scars of frostbite. Some believe that they froze to death and now search for the stoves that once littered the landscape. One of these translucent figures has been caught on camera standing in an archway. If this picture is authentic, then it serves as the most substantial proof of the island's spectral inhabitants.

Oddly enough, one of Fort Delaware's many ghosts is a Union guard who patrols the ramparts.

Other ghosts, whose figures are just as fleeting, but who do not bear the signs of exposure, have been seen on the former site of the gothic wooden chapel that the prisoners worked so hard to build. The chapel was destroyed in a hurricane before the turn of the 20th century, but the dead remember where it once was and return there seeking the solace that had eluded them during their lives, no matter how diligently they prayed.

While traveling on boat to get to the fort, people have also reported seeing hands rise out of the water, beckoning to whoever sees them that they need help. However, before the people who have witnessed these disembodied extremities can shout out for help or throw a life preserver, the hands fade away. It is commonly agreed that these phantom fingers belong to the men who died trying to escape the island on their homemade rafts, their bodies having long ago sunk to the bottom of the river.

The Confederates, though, do not have a monopoly when it comes to the fort's supernatural phenomena. The ghostly figure of a Union soldier has also been seen walking throughout the fort, dressed in a cloak and carrying a lantern, as if on a never-ending search for the men who now beckon for help from the river. Believed to be the officer once in charge of searching for missing prisoners, this ghost seems to have taken its duties so seriously that it felt bound to complete them from beyond the grave.

Sounds have also been heard throughout the island. Most often described as the pathetic wailing of grown men, the sounds make for an extremely unnerving and disheartening experience, even more so than catching a glimpse of one of the more visible ghosts.

It isn't hard to understand why the ghosts of those imprisoned at Fort Delaware would choose to spend the afterlife reliving the agonies they suffered in life. Of all the places to die, the worst may very well be a prison. To die knowing that one is not free can be such a burden that the dead often find themselves spiritually bound to their prison, denying their souls the escape they dreamed of for so long. Some weep, some pray, some beckon and some search for warmth, but all the ghosts at Fort Delaware must forever grapple with this cruel irony. Whether they died of disease, exposure or malnutrition, these ghosts find themselves destined to spend eternity in the place that made their deaths possible. That alone is worth a millennium of tears.

Captain Clapp
PORTLAND, MAINE

It takes only a quick look at the rest of the stories in this book to see that most ghosts haunt the places where they once lived, died or suffered a grave injustice. Of course there are always exceptions to the rule. In this case the exception is the ghost of Captain Asa Clapp, who lived from 1762 to 1848. He is said to haunt not one but two different houses. Although he once owned one of the houses, he never spent more than a few nights there; in the other he was never anything more a casual guest. Why, then, would his ghost decide to roam these halls? Simple—he has nowhere else to go.

The most powerful house- and ship-builder in Maine, Captain Clapp was a shrewd businessman who made a fortune in real estate. In 1817, he bought a three-story brick house, built by a man named Hugh McLellan, which he held on to for almost eight years. He never lived in it, having made the purchase only because he was able to buy it at one-fifth its value. When he sold it to another sea captain, Joshua Wingate, he made a large profit on the deal.

Not long after the transaction, the families of Captains Clapp and Wingate were joined by marriage when Captain Clapp's son married Captain Wingate's daughter. Since his wife wanted to be close to her family, Captain Clapp's son

*The Clapp House, one of two buildings haunted by Captain Asa
Clapp*

Charles bought the land next door to his father-in-law's
new house and built a home in the Greek Revival style for
himself and his bride.

In 1848, Captain Clapp died, but almost 70 years
would pass before his ghost had cause to show itself.

Captain Clapp's widow was much younger than her
husband and lived for many years after his death. In fact,
her life as his widow lasted much longer than her life as

his wife. Perhaps this circumstance explains why she harbored little sentimentality about the possessions that she and her dead husband once shared. A devout believer in the supernatural, she was afraid that she would stay trapped on the earth if she left anything behind. To prevent this eventuality, she drafted a will with some special provisions. Upon her death, the house she and Captain Clapp once shared—which had been hers alone from 1848 on—would be dismantled, with only a plaque left to commemorate its existence. She also insisted that the large four-poster bed that they shared be torn apart and burned. The same fate was reserved for her car, a Pierce–Arrow that did not even exist at the time of her husband's death. When Mrs. Clapp died in 1920, her orders were followed to the letter, and shortly thereafter the captain's ghost started making appearances at the former homes of his son and in-laws.

There are two theories about why the captain's ghost materialized in houses in which he was never anything more than an occasional visitor. One is that the dismantling of his house left him homeless. The other is that the flippancy with which his wife decimated his legacy horrified him so much that he returned to oversee the other houses, with which he had a marginal connection.

By this time, neither house was occupied by the captain's relatives. A financial panic in 1837 had forced Clapp's son, Charles, to sell his house, and Captain Wingate died in 1880. Wingate's daughters sold his house to a wealthy couple, Lorenzo and Margaret Sweat. Margaret was an ardent patroness of the arts, and when she died in 1908 she gave the house to the Portland

The McLellan House, now the Portland Museum of Art

Society of Art. According to her will, the society was to preserve the house as a representative 19th-century home and to construct an adjoining art gallery to be named after her husband. The Clapp house, next door, was eventually turned into the Portland School of Art.

The fact that Captain Clapp was never an admirer of the arts when he was alive makes his haunting of the two homes all the more strange. No one related to him can be found in them, and none of the possessions within them were ever actually his. His appearances at the two buildings are somewhat like that of a man who knocks on a stranger's door and asks to be allowed to stay, because he was once related to someone who lived there. He really has no right to, but so far no one has been able to get him to leave.

But then would anybody remember him if he hadn't decided to knock on the doors of these two buildings? His wife ensured that his legacy was forever destroyed. With nowhere else to go and an evident desire not to be forgotten, he had little choice but to go to the last places with which he had some tenuous connection. By doing so he has succeeding in doing something many people do not: he has kept his memory alive.

The White House
WASHINGTON, DC

It is a common tactic among skeptics of the paranormal to portray believers as ignorant and uneducated. Doing so makes it easier for them to dismiss their stories as fantasies concocted by weak minds. It's not surprising, then, that many people with paranormal inclinations are vindicated by the reports of ghosts at the world's most famous address, 1600 Pennsylvania Avenue. The stories of spirits in the White House leave skeptics tongue-tied because those who have related them number among the most well-respected people in the country's history.

Anyone who has tuned in to watch the president make a speech, talk to the press or bestow an award has at some point seen the White House's famous Rose Garden. It has frequently served as a national forum for

The White House, circa 1846

great joy and terrible sorrow. Most agree that its unique beauty makes it a fitting place to honor the ideals of the American people.

It's edifying to report, then, that according to legend, the garden exists because of direct spiritual intervention. Around 1915, Edith Wilson, Woodrow Wilson's second wife, decided that she wanted to move the garden she believed had been planted by President Wilson's first wife, Ellen. What she did not know was that the garden was located in the same spot that former first lady Dolley Madison had planted her own flowers.

A famously vibrant woman who was quick to express herself whenever displeased, Dolley apparently did not lose this trait after her death. Her ghost did not take at all well to the news that the garden, which she still considered hers, was going to be moved. When the gardeners set to work, they were immediately confronted by her irate phantom. She floated in the air wearing a beautiful, flow-ing 19th-century gown and ranted at them with such furious invective that they ran away screaming. To appease the angry spirit, hundreds of roses were planted. The del-icate grace of the garden was taken as a sign that Dolley's ghost was once again content. No one has ever attempted to move the garden since.

Another famous ghost is said to reside in a room that is not part of the public tour. The Rose Room is a large comfortable apartment that is often referred to as the Queen's Room, since five different queens have stayed there throughout the years. The large bed that sits in the room is believed to have been Andrew Jackson's. Those who have been fortunate enough to sleep in this bed have reported hearing the sound of sustained bawdy laughter coming from it. Given the complex sexual history of the seventh president, many suspect that the laughter is his.

During his time in office, President Jackson became smitten with a beautiful woman named Peggy O'Neil. When her husband, a tavern owner, committed suicide (because, some believe, he couldn't stand the attention his much younger wife received from other men), President Jackson convinced his friend, John Eaton, to propose to the attractive widow. President Jackson was a widower and could have married Peggy himself, but he felt it might have a negative impact on his administration, so having her marry his good friend seemed the best option. Peggy said yes, and she and John were soon betrothed.

As a wedding present, President Jackson appointed John to his cabinet—a gift, many believe, that had more to do with keeping Peggy nearby than with the president's

Former president Andrew Jackson

faith in his friend's political acumen. Beyond the gossip of the age, there is no physical evidence that President Jackson made a cuckold of his friend, but the sound of ribald delight apparent in the Rose Room's phantom laughter is enough for many believe that the affair did occur.

The first person to see the ghost of President Jackson was first lady Mary Todd Lincoln, who adamantly insisted that he could be found swearing and walking loudly throughout the room. It wouldn't be until the Kennedy administration that another person claimed to physically encounter Old Hickory. Lillian Parks, a White House seamstress, was doing some work in the room in preparation for a visit from Queen Elizabeth II. While she sat in a chair hemming a quilt, she sensed the presence of a man behind her. She looked around the room and saw that no one could have come in without her knowing. The hairs stood up on the back of her neck as she felt a hand grab the back of her chair. Too terrified to look back, Lillian jumped up, ran out of the room and refused to go in it alone for the duration of her employment.

The East Room was designed by the White House's architect, James Hoban, to be a public audience room. Over the years, the large room has been used for dances, gatherings, after-dinner entertainment, weddings, funerals, award ceremonies, press conferences and bill signings. Usually the room is kept empty, with the exception of some artwork and a Steinway grand piano. It is also the home for the White House's oldest ghost, Abigail Adams, who had the distinction of being the first first lady to live in the famous building. The East Room was still incomplete when President Adams and his family moved into the new house. Abigail quickly decided that it was the driest room in the building and decided to hang the family's laundry inside it. Years after Abigail died, staff members claimed to see the late first lady walking through the East Room with her arms outstretched, as if carrying a load of laundry. Many believe that the presence of her ghost can be detected by the smell of soap and damp clothing in the spacious room.

Former first lady Abigail Adams, the oldest ghost in the White House

It seems appropriate that the White House's most famous ghost belongs to the president who was most intrigued by the supernatural. Thanks to the efforts of his wife Mary, Abraham Lincoln was a believer in the paranormal (he even participated in several of the séances that she held at the White House). President Lincoln had never been comfortable with the teachings of the traditional organized religions, and for a long time he was skeptical about the notion of life after death. It took the death of his son Willie for him to become interested in the spirit world.

Mary invited several psychics to the White House to hold séances in an attempt to contact Willie's spirit. Eventually these séances became a regular occurrence during the Lincolns' years at the White House. Frequently the psychics would come in contact with spirits of dead leaders who gave President Lincoln advice from beyond the grave. Some say it was the ghost of Daniel Webster, the famous lawyer, who convinced the president to pass the Emancipation Proclamation.

In 1863, a medium named Charles Shockle visited the White House and performed a levitation that left the president dumbfounded. When Shockle did it again, this time with a piano, President Lincoln ordered a congressman from Maine to sit on the piano to prove that it wasn't a trick. The congressman did as he was told and the piano continued to float in the air as he sat on it. These séances continued until 1865, when President Lincoln's term was cut short by John Wilkes Booth. Three days before he was killed, President Lincoln is said to have prophesied his assassination in a series of dreams.

Not long after his death, his ghost began to appear at the White House. It was during Harry Truman's presidency that Lincoln's bed was moved into the large cabinet room in which the assassinated leader signed the Emancipation Proclamation. The room from that point on became known as the Lincoln Bedroom and it is the

The haunted Lincoln Bedroom

place where people are most likely to catch a glimpse of the tall, lanky phantom. Among those who have admitted to seeing or sensing the presence of President Lincoln's ghost are some of the most famous and important men and women in the 20th century. Theodore Roosevelt, Eleanor Roosevelt, Winston Churchill, Harry Truman and his wife Margaret, Dwight Eisenhower, Jacqueline Kennedy and Ladybird Johnson all claimed to have made some sort of contact with Lincoln's spirit.

Lincoln, however, is not content to appear solely in front of the White House's most important occupants. He also appears in front of the staff and any visitors lucky enough to get to spend the night in his famous room. Franklin Roosevelt's personal valet once ran out of the White House screaming when he saw the famous spirit. Mrs. Roosevelt's maid proved more courageous when she opened a door and saw President Lincoln sitting on his bed pulling off his boots. Ronald Reagan's daughter Maureen once caught a glimpse of Lincoln's translucent form while she and her husband, Dennis, were getting ready to go to bed. President Reagan admitted that he never saw the ghost himself, but that his dog, Rex, would frequently start barking whenever he passed the empty room. Queen Wilhelmina of the Netherlands remains the only member of royalty to see the ghost. She was so shocked by his sudden appearance in a doorway that she fainted where she stood.

It makes sense that throughout the White House's long history it would collect its share of spirits. No other house in America comes close to matching it in terms of history. In its time, it has been home to the most powerful men in the world, and it is because of them that the building is the national treasure it is today. Their testimonies are proof, much to the skeptic's chagrin, that with an open mind even the most intelligent person can affirm the existence of ghosts.

The Mathias Ham House
DUBUQUE, IOWA

On a windy bluff above the Mississippi River in Dubuque, Iowa, there sits a foreboding five-story Victorian mansion. It was once home to one of 19th-century Iowa's most prominent families, the Hams. Made of limestone with 23 rooms and 14-foot high ceilings, the house looks like the perfect setting for a Universal Pictures horror film from the 1930s; given its history, it's surprising that it wasn't. Although the house is a museum today, it once was the site of a frightening confrontation that forever scarred the psyche of an unfortunate woman and ended the life of an evil man. Years after this violent encounter, the house was overtaken by the angry spirit of the slain scoundrel, who even today invokes his ghastly presence in an effort to exact the revenge that he failed to carry out while alive.

A family man with five children and a wife, Mathias Ham was a successful entrepreneur who made his fortune through investments in lead, lumber and shipping. Mathias' shipping interests led him to buy the parcel of land on which he built his home. From the bluff he was able to watch as the ships he owned made their way down along the Mississippi. More importantly, he was able to chart the progress of his competitors.

In 1837, Mathias built the first part of what would eventually become his mansion. This first house was a modest affair, standing only two stories with just five rooms. It stayed that way for close to 20 years, until

The Mathias Ham House in Iowa is the site of a chilling haunting.

Mathias' wife Zerelda took ill and passed away in 1856. Then, in an effort to ease his grief, Mathias proceeded to add on to the small building, transforming it from a modest home into an immaculate wonder. While this construction took place, Mathias, who felt incomplete without a wife, married Margaret McLean, whose reputation as a gold digger was proven unfounded when she stayed with Mathias after the great financial crash of 1857 robbed him of most of his holdings. Having just completed construction of his stately new home, Mathias struggled to keep his family from facing eviction. Although he managed to keep the house, he spent the rest of his life trying to regain the fortune he lost.

Even after he lost control of his shipping company, Mathias still took great delight in watching the ships as they sailed along the mighty Mississippi. He found that charting the progress of the different boats relaxed him and kept his mind from being overcome by his financial difficulties. One day, Mathias saw a strange ship on the water. Unlike the ships he was accustomed to seeing, this vessel looked unsteady and battle worn. Mathias was shocked when he saw it suddenly attack a shipping vessel it passed along the way—the first time in many years of ship watching that he had witnessed an act of piracy.

Mathias quickly mounted his horse and raced to the house of the local constable. Together they returned to the bluff, so they could both see the pirate's boat. Thanks to the bluff's ideal vantage point, the constable was able to study the ship in detail and correctly guess where it headed after the robbery was completed. The police were easily able to catch the pirates. During the short trial that followed, Mathias was offered up as the head witness, and his testimony led to serious jail terms for all those indicted. One of them, an angry mass of tattooed muscle named McTeague, was dragged away swearing revenge on the man who testified against him. Mathias was unaffected by the man's oaths, certain that the man would never live long enough to see the end of his jail term.

Mathias was never able to recover the wealth he once possessed, yet he still led a happy life after the crash. He fathered two children with Margaret and spent the last years of his life as a doting father. Margaret died in 1874, leaving Mathias to spend the last 15 years of his life as a widower. Although he lacked the funds to distract him from the grief he felt, as he had done when his first wife died, he managed to stay cheerful for the sake of his children. By the time he died in 1889, his youngest daughter from his first marriage, Sarah, was the only family member still living with him in the large mansion.

Mathias left the house to Sarah in his will. Not wealthy enough to employ servants, Sarah had all of the house's 23 rooms to herself, which at times could be a spiritual burden. With the house's high ceilings and ornate furniture, it wasn't unusual for an unsettling eeriness to affect the atmosphere in the five-story building. Hemmed in by a deafening silence, Sarah often found it difficult to go to sleep at night.

Thanks to this paranoia-induced insomnia, Sarah often spent her nights in bed with a book to help her pass the late hours. One night, Sarah's paranoia proved prophetic when she heard the house's silence broken by the sounds of heavy footsteps from the floors below. Sarah froze in her bed and stayed silent as she strained her ears to hear the distant thumps. The frightening sounds continued for several minutes before Sarah heard what sounded like someone exiting from a window. She jumped from her bed and looked out her bedroom window. She caught a glimpse of a large man as he ran from her front lawn out into the darkness. Sarah ran downstairs and was surprised to find that nothing seemed to be missing.

The next day, Sarah told her neighbors, an old married couple, about what had happened. She asked them why anyone would bother to break into someone's house if they didn't plan to steal anything. The husband suggested that it was possible that the intruder wasn't looking for objects to steal, but instead a person to kidnap.

"Make sure that all your doors and windows are locked tight," the old man told Sarah. "There is a good chance that *you* were what he was looking for, and he might decide to try again. If he does, put a lamp in your window. I will be able to see it from my room, and I will go out and get help."

Sarah thanked the old man and did as he told her. She made sure that every window and door was firmly locked then nervously went up to her room, taking along a small gun once owned by her father. Too anxious to sleep, Sarah had difficulty concentrating on the book she was trying to read. She sat in bed like this for close to two hours until she heard the sound of a window being broken.

This time Sarah could not keep herself from speaking.

"Who's there?" she exclaimed, her voice full of panic and fear.

She immediately realized that she had alerted the intruder to her whereabouts. She jumped out of her bed and ran to her door. Seconds after she had locked it, a large body thumped against it. Luckily, the door did not break down. Sarah ran to the lamp that she had been using to read from and placed it in her window, praying that the old man would see it as he had said.

Once again the intruder slammed against the door, this time causing the wood to crack in the middle. One or two more direct hits and the door would doubtless give way. Terrified beyond measure, Sarah grabbed the gun she had brought with her and fired two shots into the door. A horrible scream roared from the other side of the door as the bullets met their target. Still holding the gun up and ready to shoot it again, Sarah listened as the intruder slowly made his way down the hall and down the stairs. She ran to her window to see if she could see him. She didn't.

Instead, she watched as a group of her neighbors gathered on her front lawn. Still too afraid to leave her room, Sarah threw down a key to the front door. By the time they reached her room, they were sure that the intruder had left the house. They knew this because of the trail of blood that began at Sarah's bedroom door and wound its way out of the back of the house. Once they were able to convince Sarah that she was safe, the neighbors followed the trail, which ended at the bank of the river. There, collapsed on the grass, was the body of an old man whose arms bore tattoos that had been described to her by her father. McTeague's dream of revenge kept him alive long enough to get out of prison, but it wasn't strong enough for him to survive the damage caused by two bullets.

Several years after her frightening encounter, Sarah was forced to sell the house to the city for $10,000, having run out of credit with which to borrow money. The city officials, however, let her stay in the house as a caretaker, which is what she did until her death in 1921.

For 40 years after Sarah's death, the mansion sat empty as the city attempted to think of ways it could use the property. In 1964 it was decided to turn it into a museum to be run by the Dubuque County Riverboat Historical Society. The house was cleaned up and restored to its appearance when Mathias built it, but despite all the society's attention to detail there remained one crucial difference. Now the house was haunted.

Stories about a ghost at the house had long been grist for the local rumor mill. The speculation had more to do with the decades it spent sitting vacant, slowly accruing the aura of a haunted house, than it did with any real evidence. It would take the opening of the museum to prove that, in this case, the rumors were justified.

The staff at the museum quickly noticed that certain places in the house—like the stairway to the third floor—made them feel uncomfortable, as if they were being watched. People who stood in these spots would often feel an icy force envelop them, chilling them to the bone. They also discovered, to their bewilderment, a window that refused to stay closed. No matter how many times a staff member shut and locked the window, it would be found, sometimes only minutes later, once again open.

As more attention was paid to these supernatural phenomena, people began to notice a strange light that coursed through the house at night. Slow and methodical, this floating illumination moved as though it was searching for something. It didn't take long for people to speculate that the dead pirate who had met an untimely end while trying to honor his vow of revenge had returned to the house to finish the job he had started. This would explain the extreme hostility that emanated from the phantom's presence. It would also explain the sudden outbursts that have become a frequent event at the museum.

A good example is the time the museum's assistant curator was startled by the loud strangled moan of a pump organ while she was switching off the front room's lights. The agonizing sound stopped when she switched the lights back on. She immediately walked over to where the pump organ sat in the house and observed that it was unchanged from when she last saw it—that is, broken and closed up. The young woman left the house with the lights on, figuring that the spirit who created the ruckus didn't want to spend that night searching in the dark.

Over the years, the museum's staff have developed a somewhat blasé attitude when it comes to their unhappy specter. Despite his menacing presence, it has become obvious that his bark is entirely without bite. McTeague, it turns out, is just a much a failure as a ghost as he was as a pirate and avenger.

It is impossible to feel any pity for such a pathetic creature. While it is a fact that two generations of Hams spoiled his evil plans, little seems to justify his presence at their former home. McTeague is foolish to blame the people who ensnared him while leading a life of crime and violence. In the end, neither Mathias nor Sarah keeps the pigheaded pirate attached to the Mathias Ham House. He can leave at any time; he's just too stupid to do so.

Goddess of Fire
MAUNA LOA, HAWAII

Despite the fear and mistrust of fundamentalists, there is an unequivocal link between the world of the supernatural and the religious. Both depend on the idea of a life beyond the physical realm and both require a leap of faith to cross the line between skepticism and belief. Because of this connection, some believe the gods of ancient religions were not simply figureheads to whom their worshippers prayed and sacrificed, but beings that bridged the divide between the physical and spiritual realm.

According to this theory, these gods were able to flourish so long as they were worshipped. It was belief that kept them alive, and when that belief faded, the gods faded with it. Thanks to the work of missionaries and others, many of these gods were wiped out in the name of Christianity, Islam and all the other major world religions. Some, however, were able to survive this onslaught and continued to live, if slightly more marginally, in the minds of their people.

One of these survivors is the goddess of the world's largest volcano, Mauna Loa, on the island of Hawaii. Her name is Pele, but she is also known as She-Who-Shapes-the-Sacred-Land. A goddess of fire, her will is often destructive and controlled by her passions. Her temper is legendary, since it often takes lives when it flares up. Over the last few years, Pele has been a relatively benign god. Her last eruption occurred in 1983. That does not mean, however, that she has ceased to exist. She appears

Mauna Loa, a massive volcano invested with mythic significance by indigenous Hawaiians

frequently on the island, taking the form of both a young woman and an old woman. She is almost always accompanied by a small white dog, which has also been known to appear by itself when it so desires.

Hawaii was not Pele's first home. The daughter of the spirit Haumea, and a direct descendent of the supreme beings Papa (Earth Mother) and Wakea (Sky Father), Pele first landed on the island of Kauai. She was pursued by her vengeful sister, Na-maka-o-kaha'i, whose husband had been seduced by the amorous Pele. Every time she attempted to dig a pit to live in (by thrusting her walking stick into the earth), the hole would be flooded by the water that Na-mako-o-kaha'i controlled in her role as queen of the sea. In an attempt to escape her angry sister's wraith, Pele traveled from island to island, until finally she reached Hawaii. It was here that she found Mauna Loa, which rose so far from the ground that not even her sister could raise the sea high enough to reach it. Pele settled on Mauna Loa's Kilauea Volcano and thrust her walking stick into the earth and formed the Halemaumau Crater, which became her home.

From its base underneath the ocean to its peak, 13,448 feet above sea level, Mauna Loa rises half a mile higher than Mount Everest, whose famous reputation is based on its elevation rather than its height. Nearby Mauna Kea is even higher, at about 13,800 feet above sea level, but its overall mass cannot compare to the massive Mauna Loa, which is made up of over 9700 cubic miles of stone and earth. Any goddess of fire would be hard pressed to find a more worthy volcano to call home.

Once Pele established herself as Mauna Loa's volatile mistress, she proceeded to use the power of the volcano's deadly magma to enforce her capricious will against the island's mortal inhabitants. What Pele did to her sister Hi'iaka and a mortal chief named Lohi'au is indicative. Hi'iaka was Pele's favorite sister, having been hatched from an egg Pele kept warm during her journey to Hawaii. Together they, along with their other sister, Laka, served as patronesses of the dance. It was in this capacity that Pele traveled back to Kauai, where a dance performance was being held. Once she arrived on the island, she took the form of a beautiful woman. While in this disguise she met and fell in love with a strong young chief named Lohi'au, who was instantly captivated by her beauty and returned her love tenfold. As much as she adored her handsome lover, Pele knew that she had to return to her real body, which was sleeping peacefully in the Halemaumau Crater. Without explaining any of this to Lohi'au, she left Kauai and returned to Hawaii. Once she awoke, she called for Hi'iaka to come to her. When her younger sister arrived, Pele explained why she had sent for her.

"There is a man on Kauai," Pele told her sister. "His name is Lohi'au, and in all my many years I have never met a man as strong and as handsome. You are to go to him and convince him to leave his people and come to me."

Unaccustomed to commands from her big sister, Hi'iaka tried to turn the situation to her advantage.

"If he is so strong and handsome," she asked her sister, "then why should I send him to you when I can have him for myself?"

Pele was angered by her sister's impertinence, but knew she needed her too much to punish her. Instead, she decided to offer up a trade.

"I have noticed you dancing with your friend Hopoe in a grove of beautiful ohi'a trees." Pele smiled wickedly. "It would be a shame if that grove were consumed in a blaze of fire."

Hi'iaka's faced paled when she heard her sister's threat.

Pele continued.

"If you convince Lohi'au to come to me without entic-
ing him yourself, then I think I can ensure that such a disaster never occurs."

Agreeing immediately to help her sister, Hi'iaka traveled to Kauai, only to find that Lohi'au had been so upset
by his love's unexplained disappearance that he had
taken ill and died. Luckily, young Hi'iaka had the power
to return his spirit to his body. The process took some
time. When the young chief finally awoke, he was overjoyed to discover that his love was still alive and waiting
for him in Hawaii. He and Hi'iaka took to the sea and
journeyed to the Big Island. What they did not know was
that after 40 days had passed Pele had become convinced
that her sister had decided to keep Lohi'au for herself.
With a vengeful fury she rained fire and lava on the ohi'a
grove, destroying the trees and killing Hi'iaka's friend
Hopoe in the process.

When Hi'iaka and Lohi'au reached Hawaii, they traveled to Mauna Loa and came across the charred ashes of
the grove along the way. Hi'iaka's grief became intolerable
when she came across the burnt remains of her friend.
Having nowhere else to turn, she threw herself into
Lohi'au's arms and wept uncontrollably. From up in her
crater, Pele saw the embrace and was convinced that it
confirmed her suspicions. With a scream of primal ferocity she sent forth another blaze of fire and lava, killing the
mortal Lohi'au and compounding Hi'iaka's grief.

Luckily for the two, the event was witnessed by Pele's
and Hi'iaka's brother, Kane-milo-hai, who snatched
Lohi'au's departing spirit out of the water and brought the
young chief back to life. No longer in love with the violent

Pele, Lohi'au asked Hi'iaka to live with him on Kauai. She accepted, much to the chagrin of her older sister.

Along with inspiring Pele's jealousy, mortals risk becoming a victim of her wrath in other ways—by stealing rocks from the Halemaumau Crater and by eating the ohelo berries that grow along her volcanic domain without asking permission and first offering her a taste. Christian missionaries deliberately broke these rules, intent as they were on showing the island's natives the irrationality of their superstitions. The Hawaiians, however, refused to defy the angry goddess since they were aware, better than anyone, of the fiery power that she possesses.

Recently Pele has returned to the public eye. In 1996, the popular musician Tori Amos released an album called *Boys for Pele*, whose title reiterated that young men in fact were sacrificed to the volcano goddess—and not the virginal young women so often presented in B-movies and pulp fiction. Pele has also been seen on the island, dressed in a red muumuu and followed by a small white dog of no fixed breed. Among the places where she has appeared are the Honolulu Hilton and at her home in Mauna Loa. Seen almost as frequently is her dog, who, when seen without its master, is said to be an omen of disaster.

In 1959, the staff of the Mauna Loa Observatory noticed that a small white mutt was foraging for food from their garbage. Attempts were made to befriend and capture the dog, but no one could even come close to snaring him. When the dog finally disappeared, the scientists were too busy dealing with the eruption of Kilauea Iki to notice. From that point on, the dog appeared and reappeared until 1961. The staff at the observatory stopped acknowledging its existence when it became clear that outsiders considered their stories about him to be uncomfortably irrational.

Perhaps Pele's destructive power has kept her from joining her fellow gods as they faded away into the past. Unlike other gods, whose presence could be dismissed in the face of contradictory evidence, she remains an ever-present factor in the lives of the Hawaiian people. As long as she controls the deadly magma that bubbles in Mauna Loa's core, there will be enough believers to keep her alive. After all, to believe in Pele is to beg for her mercy, without which the islanders would be lost.

The Wythe House
COLONIAL WILLIAMSBURG, VIRGINIA

Because Americans have long been drawn to the idea of life after death, they often believe that any house older than 100 years must be haunted. Of course this is not always the case, but it is hard not to think of ghosts when walking through houses from earlier eras. The sense of history one feels almost demands an antique spirit to accompany the antique furniture. As a consequence, the story of Anne Skipworth and her haunting of the Wythe House persists to this day, although the people who work at the Colonial Williamsburg historical park in Virginia are quick to deny it.

Founded at the beginning of the 18th century, Williamsburg was designed to be Virginia's capital. As a result, it immediately became a hub of great activity and attracted many of the important people of the era. Chief

The Wythe House in Colonial Williamsburg, Virginia

among them was George Wythe, a lawyer and teacher. Wythe's most famous pupil was none other than Thomas Jefferson, who so admired his wise professor that he requested his aid in the fight for American independence. Wythe had been drawn to Williamsburg by an offer to teach law at the College of William and Mary, a position which made him the first law professor in the United States. Richard Taliaferro, Wythe's father-in-law, was a renowned builder and planter and, as a gift to his daugh ter and her husband, he built them one of the finest homes in Williamsburg.

A two-story brick house with eight rooms, the Wythe House (as it soon became known) was the perfect model of colonial architecture. During the American Revolutionary War, the house served as headquarters for George Washington before the Siege of Yorktown and was used as accommodations by Thomas Jefferson and his family. George Wythe's place in American history was assured when, as a member of the Continental Congress, he signed the Declaration of Independence, drafted by his famous pupil. In 1780, Richmond became the new state capital, and the widowed Wythe moved there in 1791. No longer the center of political activity, Williamsburg slowly evolved into a inconsequential small town until a young Methodist reverend took notice of its grand architecture and set out to restore it to its former grandeur.

Reverend W.A.R. Goodwin's mission began in 1903 when he took over as rector of Williamsburg's Bruton Parish Church and decided to restore the church to its former glory. When the job was finished, the reverend took a job at a parish in Rochester, New York, but he never forgot the small town of Williamsburg and the history that hid inside it.

In 1923 he returned to Williamsburg and found, to his horror, that the town had sunk even deeper into a depressing state of concrete modernity. Incensed, he started a crusade to restore the town back to the colonial treasure it once was. Aided by the financial patronage of John D. Rockefeller, Jr., the reverend hired an architect named William Perry and began to buy properties along Duke of Gloucester Street. Among those he purchased was the Wythe House, which the reverend used as his residence. In 1928 Reverend Goodwin publicly made his intentions and chief benefactor known. Construction then began. Six hundred non-period buildings were destroyed, 88 original houses were restored and 500 buildings were completely reconstructed.

Reverend Goodwin knew that history alone would not be enough to attract visitors to the rebuilt Williamsburg. Once it was completed, he took to insisting that Williamsburg was an area rife with spirits in the hope that this would interest a supernaturally minded public. One of the houses that the reverend claimed was haunted was the one in which he lived. On account of his efforts, the story of Anne Skipworth and her haunting of the Wythe House became a well-known and oft-repeated story.

According to the story, Anne was the beautiful but emotionally unstable wife of Sir Peyton Skipworth, about whom little is known. The couple lived on Sir Skipworth's plantation in Mecklenburg County and only traveled to Williamsburg when the courts were in session. For reasons that are unclear, during these visits Anne stayed at the Wythe House as a guest while her husband lodged at a local tavern. One year, during such a stay, the couple was invited to a ball at the governor's mansion. Anne wore an exquisite satin gown and a pair of ornate red slippers.

Around that time rumors began to spread that Sir Skipworth was having an affair with Anne's sister, Jean. While at the governor's ball, Anne overheard a woman whisper that she had seen Sir Skipworth and Jean together a few days earlier. Shocked by this news, Anne confronted her husband, who reacted violently to the impertinence of her accusation. Tear-stricken, Anne ran from the ball, and,

George Wythe, an important lawyer and teacher, was the first to inhabit the Wythe House.

like Cinderella, lost one of her red slippers along the way. With her one remaining shoe she returned to nearby Wythe House and retired to her room, where she killed herself in a fit of despair. At night, the story goes, one can hear the sound of a single high-heeled slipper walking up and down the steps of the house's stairway. This audible evidence of Anne's ghost is said to be compounded by unnatural drafts and unexplainable cold spots—attributes that are commonly associated with the paranormal.

Unfortunately, not everyone believes the story—not even the current staff of Wythe House. They insist that the story of Anne and her one shoe is completely fictional, and that historical records prove that Anne Skipworth did not commit suicide, but died during childbirth. Those who believe the story are quick to point out that, as a matter of honor, it wasn't uncommon for a doctor to put a less scandalous cause of death on the certificate, especially when a suicide was involved. Another historical document serves as strong evidence on the side of the believers. It is the marriage certificate of Sir Skipworth and Anne's sister, Jean. The date on this document proves that they married only a few weeks after Anne's death.

While the staff at the Wythe House are adamant in their denial of Anne's ghost, labeling it a foolish story that detracts from the house's genuine historical importance, the fact is that people report hearing (and even seeing) her several times each year. In some cases, visitors have claimed to capture an eerie glow on the stairs in their snapshots. While there is a chance that the staff is right and these reports are the result of nothing more than overactive imaginations, it is also possible that the staff refuse to acknowledge Anne's existence because it might attract to the house visitors who have little respect for its real historical value. Given the many great people and events that the house was host to, perhaps their stance is not unreasonable.

6
Southern Spirits

The Eternal Party
SAVANNAH, GEORGIA

Panache is a French word that means "the ability to wear a feather in your cap." It is used to describe people who have an uncommon mixture of style and confidence. The citizens of Savannah, Georgia, brim forth with panache. There is a sense of celebration in their bearing that makes every day worth cherishing. Even in the face of great tragedy they refuse to succumb to pessimism. Nowhere is this more evident than at the Bonaventure Cemetery, where spirits gather to celebrate a moment that perfectly defined the style and grace of the people from such an extraordinary place.

Savannah was founded in 1733 by a British general named James Oglethorpe. A man of vision, the general devised a layout for his city that would make it unique in North America. What he created is a system of 23 squares that serve as miniature parks. Each square is surrounded by houses, churches and businesses, all of which are designed to give their particular square a unique personality.

Few cities can compete with Savannah when it comes to architectural beauty. Over the years a number of film productions have flocked to the city, including crews for the blockbuster hits *Forrest Gump* and *The General's Daughter*, as well as the landmark television mini-series *Roots*. Also filmed in Savannah was the Clint Eastwood-directed *Midnight in the Garden of Good and Evil*, based on John Berendt's bestseller. The book, which was published to little acclaim but became a word-of-mouth

Statue of Savannah founder James Oglethorpe

literary sensation, has put Savannah in the spotlight in recent years. Yet even prior to the book's publication, the city was often referred to as the Hostess City of the South on account of its reputation for hospitality and old-fashioned southern gentility. Needless to say, Savannah is a very popular tourist destination today, and the

Bonaventure Cemetery must be one of its most fascinat
ing historical attractions.

The cemetery sits on the grounds of what used to be a
beautiful plantation. The land was owned by a British
colonel named Mulryne, who remained loyal to King
George even as the threat of revolution rumbled around
him. His daughter Mary married a man named Josiah
Tatnall, and the couple gave the colonel two grand-
children, John and Josiah, Jr. Together they lived on the
plantation, until at last the threat of war made their staying intolerable. They left for England, but not everyone
was happy about it.

Josiah, Jr., did not share his family's affinity for the
mad king. He had been born in the colonies and felt more
loyal to them than he did to a foreign land his parents
insisted he call home. Like his colonial compatriots, he
rebelled—not just against his family but his king as well.
He left England and returned home to fight against the
British soldiers his family supported. A brave man, he
gained the respect of his peers and soon became a well-
known and well-liked figure in Georgia.

After the war was over, Josiah, Jr., took possession of
his family's plantation and made it his home. The three-
story house on the property was named The Bonaventure,
a combination of the Italian words *buono* ("good") and
ventura ("fortune"). When Colonel Mulryne built it, he
had insisted that it be constructed entirely out of brick
imported from England. As a result, the home became
somewhat unique in the history of southern plantation
architecture, in which the tendency was in favor of lighter
and less durable materials.

The Bonaventure's exterior had the same lofty atmosphere of a British manor house. Its design was meant to intimidate the lower classes and instill in them a respect towards their so-called betters. This always made Josiah slightly uneasy, so with the help of his wife Harriet he made an effort to make the interior as comfortable as possible.

Each room was decorated to please the eye, but also—more importantly—to make visitors feel at home. Despite his wealth, Josiah refused to sacrifice his home's coziness for any kind of ostentation. His furnishings were always beautiful without being ornate. Guests who stayed at the Bonaventure often expressed grief at having to leave it. The combination of the house's welcoming atmosphere and its host's generosity made it the type of place where one could willingly spend a lifetime.

For a time Josiah's life at the Bonaventure truly was full of good fortune. He greatly increased his wealth by growing cotton and he began to dabble in politics. His dabbling led to his serving briefly as both a congressman and as governor of Georgia. His tenure in both offices proved uneventful, but he enjoyed them immensely. After these experiments in public service, Josiah was content to stay at home and tend to local matters in Savannah. He and Harriet organized lavish dinner parties with neighbors and other members of Savannah's elite.

By far the most memorable of these parties was thrown late one November. It was the last party ever held at the Bonaventure, and all the people who were lucky enough to be there have never really left it.

Like Josiah and Harriet's previous parties, this one began with their guests arriving by boat and carriage. They

Sounds of wine glasses crashing against trees recur on the former grounds—a ghostly remnant of a dramatic dinner party.

wore their finest clothes, as the Tatnalls' parties were always formal affairs. As the visitors walked along the grounds, they saw that the trees were festooned with glowing lanterns. The guests were greeted at the door by Josiah and Harriet and led by a butler to a large living room where costumed servants served wine and hors d'oeuvres. As the guests mingled they made comments about how beautifully the house had been decorated for the party. Greenery from the garden was hung throughout and the fireplace gave the room a lovely incandescent glow. When everyone had arrived, the Tatnalls joined their guests in the living room and entertained until their butler arrived and informed everyone that dinner was ready to be served.

The guests entered the Bonaventure's large dining room, which contained the one piece of furniture that belied the Tatnalls' wealth—an oak table large enough to seat a small army. The guests sat in the spots that Harriet had assigned to them, and they were delighted to discover that each of them had a servant of their own for the duration of the meal.

The meal included courses of ham, wild duck, oyster casserole and turkey. The conversation never stopped, and Josiah was delighted by the party's lively atmosphere. He was about to ask the woman who sat to his right how her young daughter was when his butler appeared behind him and whispered in his ear.

"I am sorry to interrupt you, sir." If there was panic in the butler's voice, it was because he feared disturbing his master more then anything else. "But I am afraid that a fire has broken out on the roof. We have tried to take care of it, but our efforts have failed. I'm afraid evacuation is our only recourse."

Josiah looked at the man and saw in his eyes that he spoke the truth. He calmly nodded and stood up from his chair. He picked up his glass and his knife and got everyone's attention by clinking them together.

"I am sorry to interrupt your conversations, but I have just been informed that the house is on fire. It is in our best interest to leave before we risk injury." He did not give his guests enough time to react before he spoke again. "So I ask you all to grab hold of your plates and follow me out to the garden." He then turned to his butler. "We will need some place to sit and eat. Have your men follow us out with the table and chairs." His butler nodded and Josiah, Jr., lifted up his plate, glass and cutlery and calmly walked out of his house. His guests, soothed by their host's sanguine reaction, calmly followed him; they in turn were followed by the servants who carried the dining room furniture with them.

When the table and chairs were set out in the garden, Josiah, Harriet and all their guests sat back down in their places. As the fire began to rage, Josiah entertained his guests with amusing anecdotes from his past. His natural ebullience was enough to distract his guests from dwelling on the rather conspicuous misfortune that was unfolding behind them as he spoke.

"Do you know that this isn't the first time fire has seen fit to attack us at the Bonaventure? God's honest truth. Just three months ago I was saved by the quick-thinking of one of our maids. You see the morning had just arrived and I was not yet dressed. It was chilly, unseasonably so. I had Matthew start a fire in my hearth, and I stood in front of it to warm my bones. Harriet came in to say good morning and I turned to greet her, and as I did the back of my robe flew into the hearth. Neither of us noticed as we talked that it had ignited and was on fire! I felt the heat on the back of my legs, but I assumed that was merely the result of my being so close to the fireplace. It was only when Lucy, one of our maids, walked into the room that someone realized I was aflame! It turned out the Lord was looking out for me that morning, for the reason Lucy had walked into my room was to water the plants. When she saw the state I was in, she screamed and threw the entire jug of water on me.

The water was cold and shocked me something fierce. I turned and was ready to give Lucy a furious tongue-lashing, when Harriet saw the smoking remains of the back of my robe and screamed herself. If it were not for Lucy I would not be here today to tell you this story."

Everyone smiled at this and Josiah was about to remark that it was a pity that Lucy wasn't available with her trusty water jug right now, when a good friend of his politely coughed and stood up.

"Forgive me for interrupting you, Josiah, but as this has been a beautiful night I cannot help but feel that I would be remiss if I did not raise my glass to you and thank you for inviting us all here this evening." He took a drink from his glass. In the silence of the moment there was only the sound of the crackling fire. This inspired more words from Josiah's friend. "I would also like to say that those flames take with them a home that I will never see replicated again. Its beauty was matched only by its comfort." With that he sat down.

Before Josiah could thank him for his kind words, another guest rose and offered up similar toasts to the Bonaventure, the Tatnalls' generosity and the fine meal they served. When the man finished, he was followed by another guest and in turn everyone who sat around the table did the same. The servants who stood behind them remained silent, steadfast in their duty, but tears were spied falling down their cheeks, so moved were they by the moment's perfection.

As affected as his servants, Josiah stood and drank down the contents of his glass. The glass was a rich detailed crystal, imported from France and very expensive.

Today, the atmospheric Bonaventure Cemetery stands where the Tatnalls' grand house burned to the ground.

It occurred to Josiah that the glass was one of his last remaining possessions. With a smile on his face he stood up and hurled it against a nearby tree. With happy tears falling down her face, Harriet drank down her wine and threw her glass as well. Everyone laughed and the guests took turns finishing their drinks and throwing their glasses against the tree. The sound of their laughter and of the breaking glass echoed through the night.

Two centuries have passed since then, but the panache showed by Josiah Tatnall and his guests lives on. Those who have been in the cemetery at night have heard the sounds of their laughter and of their glasses smashing against the trees. Having experienced a moment of sublime distinction, little wonder that they could think of no better way to spend eternity then to relive it each night.

The ghosts of Bonaventure Cemetery ideally reflect the flair of Savannah. Unlike other spirits, they haunt the earth not to mourn or revenge; they stay because they can think of no other place that would seem as perfect.

River of Blood
CHATTANOOGA, TENNESSEE

There is an unspoken rule in comedy that words with K sounds in them are inherently funny. Chickamauga is no exception to this rule. Those who would try to guess the word's meaning would probably assume that it describes a person or event that is amiably goofy. The truth is, this friendly sounding word is Cherokee for "river of blood"— a translation which perfectly suits the land which it names.

Located in the Georgia Mountains, close to the town of Chattanooga, Tennessee, the land that is now known as the Chickamauga Military Park was once the site of one of the deadliest battles of the Civil War. It lasted three days in September 1863. At the end of it, 35,000 of the 120,000 who fought were dead. Enough blood had been spilt for the land's name to become a literal reality. The blood

Fort Chickamauga Military Park, Chattanooga, Tennessee

flowed like a river and fed the earth, imbuing it with the spirit of the fallen. After so much carnage, it would be impossible for the now-quiet land not to bear traces of the supernatural, but many believe that the land was cursed long before it knew the tragedy of war.

The first thing people notice is the fog. It is heavy and thick, like a great billow of smoke. It comes only at night and cannot be seen from a distance. Often people won't even be aware of it until they have been swallowed by it, and then it becomes difficult to be aware of anything else. Few people are satisfied with the scientific explanations for this blanket of white mist, so they offer up their own interpretations.

Some believe that during the battle the land swallowed the smoke of the cannons and rifles, inhaling it to allow those who continued the slaughter to witness the horror of their actions. Today, the land exhales the smoke back out at night to remind the living of that same horror. Others believe that the fog is a great mass of connected spirits. These dead soldiers, they say, are not satisfied appearing alone, where the wisps of their souls risk going unnoticed, so instead they arise as one, ignoring the division of Rebel and Yankee, and cover the ground with such a density that they are impossible to ignore. There are also those, however, who insist that the opposite is true—that the ghosts of the dead do not want to be seen and that they bring up the fog so they can move freely without being spotted. Whatever the case, the fog remains.

Along with the fog are sounds that belong to neither day nor night and that have no earthly reason for being. The sounds of cannons blasting, gunshots firing and the wounded moaning have been heard by visitors and park rangers alike. These eerie reminders of the field's bloody past are too distinct to be shrugged off as the work of the park's guests. While the sound of a car backfiring is loud and unpleasant, only the most narrow-minded skeptic could confuse it for the unmistakable sound of exploding gunpowder.

Even more palpable than these sounds from the past is the ghost of a woman who has been seen walking throughout the park each year during September. Given her description, she seems to be the spiritual opposite of another Civil War ghost, Melanie Lanier, the Lady in Black who once haunted the soldiers unfortunate enough to be posted at Boston Harbor's Fort Warren. Like Melanie, this ghost, whose real name is unknown, is a beautiful woman who lost her beloved in the war. Unlike Melanie, however, this ghost does not wear the grieving black of a widow, but rather the innocent white of a joyful bride. Her hair is blonde and her aspect demure.

The Lady in White does not walk the earth searching for vengeance, since there is no one left to exact it from. All she can do now is look for her fallen groom, but he is just one of 35,000, and there is a good chance that she would not even recognize him if she found him. It is possible that she will never find the peace that eventually allowed the Lady in Black to move on, but as long as she has time she has a chance.

Which is more than can be said for anyone unfortunate enough to run into the park's most famous supernatural resident, a creature so loathsome that many consider it not a ghost but a demon from hell. There are many different legends associated with the frightening monster known as Old Green Eyes. One claims that it is the ghost of a Union soldier who was killed by his own brother, who fought with the Confederacy. Some who tell the story go as far to claim that Old Green Eyes doesn't actually have a body. As they tell it, his head was all that could be found after the battle. It was buried, but it soon

Inexplicable battlefield sounds serve as a haunting reminder of the park's bloody past.

emerged from the grave in search of the body it lost. They claim it can be seen floating in the dark, thanks to the light from its horrible glowing green eyes.

Those, however, who have actually seen the beast insist that it does have a body. Its arms, legs and torso are that of a man, but all human similarities end there. Its hair is a long and tangled mess, dyed red from the blood of its victims. Its eyes are a queasy orangish-green—an unsettling combination of fire and rot—and its teeth are sharp and jagged, capable of easily tearing out a person's throat. It walks the earth naked, save for a long black cape that always flies throughout the air, regardless of whether the wind is strong enough to lift it.

Those lucky enough to have survived their encounter with the beast insist that Old Green Eyes is a creature of palpable flesh and blood. They believe the rumors that it existed long before the Civil War, and that it may have had a hand in the battle's horrible body count. Over the last three decades, at least two car accidents have been directly attributed to this possible demon. In both cases the drivers were so shocked and frightened by the sudden appearance of two glowing green eyes in the dark that they swerved off the road into a tree. Given many people's reticence in relating their encounters with the unknown, it isn't a stretch to consider that several similar accidents have since gone unrecorded.

Another bizarre story, possibly related to Old Green Eyes, took place during the summer of 1970. A group of teenagers, emboldened by alcohol and taunting, drove down to the park in the hopes of seeing one of its famous spirits. While they drunkenly searched around the park they came across a tower built in 1903 as a memorial to Colonel John Wilder, a Union officer whose generosity and bravery had greatly touched the men who served under him. The stone tower was 85 feet high and equipped with gun turrets to honor Colonel Wilder's $25,000 contribution to supply his troops with rifles for the horrendous battle.

Slightly amazed by the novelty of the structure, the teenagers spent some time egging each other on to find a way to get inside, so they could do some exploring. Finally, one of them noticed the lightning rod that was attached to the side of the tower. He shinnied up the steel pole and noticed an open gun turret about 14 feet up. He squeezed himself through the small aperture and shouted down to his friends to join him. They began to do just that when they were interrupted by a scream of such abject terror it froze them where they stood. To their horror, they watched as their friend inside the tower made a horrible miscalculation. In his desperate effort to flee from whatever it was that he saw, he ran to what he thought was the same window from which he entered. He discovered, a little too late, that the lightning rod was not there. He plunged 25 feet down onto hard concrete. He survived the fall, but would never walk again. He refused to ever talk about what it was that had so terrified him that night, but many assume that he ran into Old Green Eyes, who some have suggested may now use the tower as its home.

The tower was also the site of another strange occurrence in 1976. During the stone building's construction, the men who had served under Colonel Wilder collected a selection of important Civil War artifacts and sealed them behind a cornerstone. They wanted the stone to be removed at a future date for a future generation to appreciate. Seventy-four years later it was decided that the American bicentennial was the perfect time to retrieve these historic souvenirs. The ceremony began with the typical mixture of speeches and songs, but it quickly turned sour when the cornerstone was removed and revealed nothing but a big empty space. Contrary to all

228 Ghost Stories of America Vol. II

logical assumptions, no evidence of theft or tampering could be found. It appeared that everything had just vanished into thin air. Again, some attributed the disappearance to Old Green Eyes, while others believed that the mementos had simply been taken back by the ghosts of the men who had left them.

Over a century after the river of blood stopped flowing, the ghosts of the Chickamauga Military Park have yet to forget the bloodshed that tied them to the land. Because it seems unlikely that any one event will allow them to pass over to the other side, there is a good chance that park visitors will see a strange fog, a pair of menacing green eyes or (if they visit in September) a beautiful bride in search of her missing groom. But then, perhaps, it might be better if they didn't.

The Nutt House
NATCHEZ, MISSISSIPPI

By an unfortunate accident of birth, a man capable of grandiose visions and vibrant imagination was saddled with the last name of Nutt. But Dr. Haller Nutt was not a kook or a loon. A passionate and intelligent man who dreamed of owning a house that was unique, he spent a great deal of money trying to make his dream come to fruition. Unfortunately, the realities of life in the 1860s shattered his hopes. He died a broken man, still dreaming of the house that he so passionately believed in. For a long time after his death, the house was called "Nutt's Folly," but, as is so often the case in stories like these, time has

The Nutt House, Natchez, Mississippi

vindicated his vision and today people come from all over to visit his incomplete home. This would seem bittersweet if Dr. Nutt weren't so acutely aware of the attention his house now receives. Over a century may have passed since his demise, but that hasn't stopped him from greeting visitors and serving as an occasional tour guide in his vintage home.

Dr. Nutt, a clever businessman, became a millionaire before he was 30. Investing in cotton made him even wealthier, and all the more attractive to the women who moved through his social circle. Julia Williams, a bright and uncommonly beautiful young lady, was lucky enough to catch his eye; after a short courtship they were married. A devoted husband, Dr. Nutt loved to surprise his wife with unexpected gifts, some of which were larger than others. When Julia told him how much she admired her friend Mary's house—known throughout Natchez as Longwood—he took note of it. Years later, when Longwood was put up for sale, he bought it immediately. He reveled in Julia's joy when he took her into the house, on what she thought was just a visit, and asked her how she wanted it decorated.

As the years passed, the Nutt family grew to include eight children, which proved to be too many to live comfortably in Longwood. Dr. Nutt bought some land and hired an architect from Philadelphia named Samual Sloan to build a new house. Referred to as Longwood II, the house was one of the most ambitious of its kind in the country. Octagonal, six stories high with plenty of space for the finest art and furniture Europe and the Orient could supply, Longwood II would prove to be a massive undertaking.

The scope of the project worried Julia, who was afraid that her husband's dream was too big to turn into reality.

"You don't have to do this," she told him. "I'm sure we would all be happy in a more modest house."

"We would be happy in a mud hut," Dr. Nutt assured her. "We would be happy anywhere as long as we were together. I am building this house because I love you all. I have the means to build you a great monument and I intend to do so."

Julia realized that this was something her husband simply had to do, so she never questioned him again.

Two long years passed as the walls were raised and the 32 rooms were built. From the outside the house looked almost finished, but a peek at the interior proved that appearances could be deceiving. The windows and doors had yet to be installed and the walls had not been plastered or painted. The ornate woodwork Dr. Nutt had planned had yet to be carved. These were the most obvious of the 100 or so finishing touches that required attention before the art and furniture could be moved in. By this time, Dr. Nutt had already spent over $100,000 on his dream house—not much by today's standards, but at the time almost five times what similar houses usually cost.

The strain that the construction exerted on Dr. Nutt made Julia anxious. This was aggravated by delays that prevented the completion of the house in the allotted two months. A bloody war between the Northern Union and the Southern Confederacy ensured that the house would never be completed.

When the Civil War erupted, Dr. Nutt watched his architect, Sloan, and his tradesmen abandon their work and return home to join the Union army. As the war began to rage, Dr. Nutt and his family took refuge in Longwood II's basement, the only part of the house that was inhabitable. As hard as it was on his spirit, the war proved to be an even greater burden on Dr. Nutt's finances. The fields of cotton that made him rich were either confiscated by the Union troops he sided with or burned by hostile Confederates. To make matters worse, all the fineries and antiques he had ordered from around the world were seized at federal blockades; they never made it to Longwood II.

The specter of Dr. Haller Nutt haunts his former home, whose construction was permanently interrupted by the outbreak of the Civil War.

In total, the Nutt family spent three years living in the basement. Julia and her children were helpless as they watched the man they loved become overwhelmed by despair.

"Remember what you told me?" Julia asked her husband one sad day. "You told me that we would be happy living in a mud hut, as long as we were together."

"This isn't a mud hut," was his terse reply.

The combination of his poverty and the unbearable proximity to his failed monument killed Dr. Nutt. The cold and damp basement infected his lungs, and the disappointment infected his mind. As pneumonia took hold of him, he felt no reason to fight it. Considering himself a man who could not even protect his own family, he welcomed death.

Almost 150 years later, the benches, buckets and scaffolding left by the workmen can still be found throughout the upper levels of the building. The Nutt family lived in the basement for years, but they could never afford to complete their father's vision. Still, knowing that it was his monument to them, when it came time for them to leave they chose not to sell the property, but instead donated it the Pilgrimage Garden Club, which maintains it to this day. Thanks to their efforts, the house is now a popular tourist attraction, and Dr. Nutt is finally able to take pleasure in his creation. At last, it has become a recognized monument of his familial devotion. Perhaps this is why he has returned to it.

The ghost of Dr. Nutt delights in appearing before people who visit his former home. He is most frequently seen in the garden area, imagining how much better the house will look when the work is finished. Despite the sadness of his story, there appears to be no melancholy in his ghostly aspect. The same holds true for the ghost of his wife Julia, who also seems to enjoy the company of visitors. She is most often spotted on the stairway, dressed in a beautiful pink dress. In her smile one can see the joy that Dr. Nutt so delighted in bringing forth. She and her husband have finally found some measure of happiness after so much misery.

Waverly Hills Sanatorium
LOUISVILLE, KENTUCKY

It is easy to forget, in this age of antibiotics and miracle drugs, how dangerous infectious diseases were once considered. Epidemics such as smallpox and scarlet fever once ran rampant throughout America, taking thousands of lives. At the beginning of the 20th century, tuberculosis (TB) did much the same. It wasn't until 1944, when Selman Waksman discovered streptomycin, that the scourge of TB was vanquished. Before then, people unfortunate enough to contract the disease required intense periods of rest and constant care to survive. Although the disease remained inactive in 90 percent of those infected, the unlucky 10 percent who did develop symptoms suffered the pain of having their organs attacked by the TB bacteria. Targeting the lungs, the bacteria killed living tissue and caused death if left untreated for too long.

The infected had to be quarantined away from the healthy since the disease spread very rapidly. To this end, hospitals and sanatoriums were built to specifically treat those with TB. One of these was the Waverly Hills Sanatorium in Louisville, Kentucky, erected in 1911. When it first opened, it had room for only 40 patients, but by 1926 it had been expanded to accommodate 400. Jefferson County had one of the country's highest rates of TB, so the Waverly almost always operated at maximum capacity. The doctors and nurses at the sanatorium were skilled at their jobs, and many of those who entered as patients eventually left the hospital with a clean bill of health.

Ghost hunters have reported many suspicious phenomena at Waverly Hills Sanatorium in Kentucky.

Many were not so lucky. According to some reports, when the TB epidemic was at its peak, the Waverly lost a patient at the rate of one an hour. Tens of thousands of men, women and children died in the castle-like hospital, so it is little wonder that the majority of visitors to the abandoned building today feel as though it emanates a strong supernatural energy.

Thanks to streptomycin, the number of patients at the Waverly rapidly declined, until the hospital was deemed unnecessary and was shut down in 1961. Two years later, it reopened as an old folks' home, where, in a situation sadly typical of the era, many elderly residents were mistreated. When, in 1980, reports of this abuse began to surface, the state decided to close down the Waverly for good. It has been empty ever since. Several attempts have been made to renovate the building, but in each case the cost of doing so has proven too exorbitant. Even those who have bought the property just for the land have discovered that to tear the building down would cost more than any future structure could recover in a reasonable amount of time.

Owners of the Waverly have often employed security guards to watch over it, but that has done little to stop the curious from sneaking in and taking an uninvited tour. Although all the doors on the lower level have been boarded shut, people still manage to get in, and they often leave with reports of paranormal activity. These trespassers are primarily responsible for the building's current dilapidated state. All its windows are broken, and it is hard to find a wall that hasn't been covered with graffiti. Not surprsingly, many describe it like something out of a horror movie—a visual cliché that makes an impressionable visitor all the more anxious.

Those who trespass into the gothic five-story building, with its long dark hallways and cold empty rooms, do so because they have heard the legends attributed to the Waverly. They have heard the story of the ghost nurse who was so emotionally tortured by the constant presence of death that she hanged herself in room 502. They may have also heard about the ghost of the elderly woman who haunts the main entrance. Blood spurts from her wrists as she begs everyone she sees for some much-needed help. Or perhaps visitors have heard about Mary, a young woman who has been seen staring out of a third-floor window. The trespassers often leave before seeing these specific ghosts, but that seldom means they leave disappointed. While these three phantoms are the Waverly's most publicized, there are many others who are not nearly as famous.

The Waverly's reputation as a haunted building is not strictly a local phenomenon. The old hospital was brought to national attention when it was featured on the Fox Family Channel show *Scariest Places on Earth*. Hosted by *The Exorcist*'s Linda Blair and shot in a style similar to the hit film *The Blair Witch Project*, the show followed a group of six young women as they walked through the old building. Not wanting to leave anything to chance, the producers of the show faked various noises and unnatural occurrences, but the women were far more frightened by the phenomena the producers had nothing to do with. One of the women, Amy Brown, heard doors slamming and saw an emaciated old man staring down at her from a second-floor window. She described feeling an eerie cold chill on her skin, and in some rooms she felt surrounded by a sea of invisible strangers. The other women described seeing images flash past doors and saw small objects move without any visible assistance.

A bizarre footnote to the filming occurred a few months later when a woman arrived at the front gates and informed the security guard on duty that she worked for the show and needed to record some sounds for the final edit. Although she appeared to have no equipment on her, the guard let her in. When the owner, Charles Mattingly, came by a few minutes later, the guard told him about the woman he let inside. Not expecting anybody that day,

Dilapidated and deserted today, the sanatorium once served as a tuberculosis clinic.

Charles called the production company that produced the show and learned that they hadn't sent anyone over there and that they had all the sounds they needed. Charles and a group of security groups went into the building to find the woman. They caught her wandering down the third floor. Charles tried to get her to leave, but instead she stepped into a room, claiming that a spirit was drawing her to it. She insisted that Charles search the room's closet; he impatiently humored her. To his shock and amazement, he found a hole in the back of the closet that contained a metal spoon, a small ladies' slipper and, most importantly, three photographs, one of which was of a pretty young woman. On the back of the photograph was the name "Mary" written in pencil. The woman left after that and was never heard from again.

With its heavy stone structure and damaged interior it is easy to understand why people are so intrigued by the Waverly. It is as close to a haunted castle as one can find in North America. It is the type of building we see in our nightmares, and its appearance is made all the more disturbing with the knowledge that so many people died within it. The Waverly Hills Sanatorium breathes and shakes with the collected energy of all the men, women and children who desperately fought against TB. Some of the spirits who suffered there feel the need to make their presence known, but just because they are more vocal doesn't mean their pain is any more horrible than those who choose to remain quiet. These silent spirits have accepted their fate and feel no need to burden the living with their torment.

The Face in the Window
CARROLLTON, ALABAMA

The citizens of Carrollton, Alabama, tried three times to build a courthouse that would last. The first building was the pride of the town, an architectural marvel that the small community had scrimped and saved to build. It was destroyed in 1865 when Union soldiers invaded the town and burned down a commissary that contained Confederate supplies. Heavily demoralized by the war and the loss, the citizens banded together to rebuild the courthouse. They wanted to restore their pride, not because they had a genuine need for it. Once again, they saved up and managed to build a courthouse that was in every way equal to its predecessor. The sense of accomplishment proved to be short lived, however, since the building fell victim to disaster in 1876. For two long years, the sheriff of Carrollton investigated the fire that destroyed the second courthouse, and during that time the town rallied once again and stubbornly built a third. This one wasn't quite as nice as the first two, but it got the job done.

Angered by the sheriff's inability to find an arson suspect, the townspeople hinted that he should find a new job. He intensified his investigation, but it was only through dumb luck that he was able to make an arrest. Bill Burkhalter was charged with assault when he inadvertently confessed that he was partly responsible for the fire. He admitted that he and another man, a former slave named Henry Wells, had broken into the courthouse in search of some money they had heard was kept inside. Bill insisted that Henry had set the fire.

"He said he didn't want no evidence to be found 'gainst him."

Henry Wells was infamous around town. His quick temper was often the cause of violence, and he had been in and out of the last two courthouses over the years on a variety of charges. He was easily found and, based solely on Bill's confession, was arrested for starting the fire. Not long after, the word spread that the arrest had been made, and an irate mob gathered in the town square.

Despite all the citizens' efforts to build a courthouse, the people of Carrollton seemed to have little use for the machinations of jurisprudence. They wanted to punish the man who had caused so much misery and they wanted to punish him immediately. Sensing that a lynch mob might take control, the sheriff moved Henry up to the courthouse's third-floor garret, where the accused had an eagle-eye view of the men and women who screamed for his blood.

The day was unusually hot for the time of year, and black clouds started to form as it became night. Henry opened up a window and shouted down to the angry crowd below.

"It wasn' me! I swear it wasn'! Bill's a liar, y'all know that! He done it!"

In response, the crowd hurled every insult they could imagine at him. Henry knew there was no convincing them that he was innocent.

"Damn y'all then! Damn y'all! If ya kill me I'll haunt y'all till the reckonin'! I swear it!" With that, he closed the

242 Ghost Stories of America Vol. II
242 **Ghost Stories of America Vol. II**

window and glared down at them. His face bore the full fruit of the fear and anger that churned inside him.

As the mob reached its boiling point, the people of Carrollton began to move towards the courthouse. A hard heavy rain began to fall out of the sky. Lightning bolts lit up the horizon, followed by the sound of their thunder. They reached the steps and were just about to break in when a flash of lightning and a clap of thunder simultaneously occurred overhead. A collective breath was held as their eyes searched the facade for flames, fearing that a fourth courthouse would soon be needed. To their great relief, the lightning appeared to do no damage. Undaunted, they resumed their quest to lynch Henry.

When they got to him, their hearts skipped a beat. They found Henry on the floor, burnt to a crisp. It was he and not the building that had suffered the full wrath of the lightning bolt. Shocked by their discovery, they were even more amazed when they looked up at the window. Etched in the glass was Henry's face, full of the same fear, anger and hatred that it bore the moment he died.

The sheriff was the first man who tried to erase the image from the window, but he found that no amount of scrubbing or solvents could remove it. Something seemed to protect that glass. Over the years, almost every window in the building has needed replacing owing to breakage caused by weather, accidents or vandals, but the window that bears Henry's image has never been damaged.

Some who have gotten close to it have claimed to see Henry's eyes staring back at them, leading many to believe that his soul is trapped there in the glass. Perhaps he is merely keeping his promise to haunt the town until the

Four Horsemen begin their apocalyptic ride. Or maybe it is his punishment for the crimes he committed against the people of Carrollton. If the latter is true, it seems a harsh sentence; if the former is true, we can only hope that Henry stays up there for a very long time.

Old-Time Politics
LITTLE ROCK, ARKANSAS

It seems appropriate that the building that once housed the Arkansas State Assembly should now itself be the subject of some debate in the city of Little Rock. At issue is not whether the building is haunted, since anyone who has walked its halls and felt the chilly air that inhabits every crevice would find it hard to argue otherwise. Instead, the debate focuses on the identity of the spirit whose gloom casts a pall on all who enter it. Some believe it is the ghost of the erstwhile Speaker of the House, who killed another representative right on the chamber's floor. Others feel it must be the ghost of the man who tried— and very nearly succeeded in—taking over the governorship in an unusual coup d'état. Both men had ample reason to return to the building after their deaths. Which one has is a question that may never be answered.

Colonel John Wilson was a banker and the speaker of the house in the Arkansas Legislature. A wealthy man, whose military service did little beyond confer a rank, he dreamed of rising up through the political ranks to the highest levels of public service. Unfortunately, his quick temper ensured that he would never reach his goal. Worse,

Wilson lost it over an insult so obscure that he was one of the only people in the room to understand it.

One day in 1837, Colonel Wilson was presiding over the assembly when Representative Amos Kuykendall brought forth a motion for a bill that would allow hunters to collect a bounty on wolf hides. While the consensus was that the bill was a good idea, a debate began about how exactly the cash-poor local magistrates could pay these bounties. After several ideas had been suggested and shot down, one representative suggested that in place of cash, hunters be given certificates.

At this point, Major J.J. Anthony, an often-belligerent representative from Randolph County, stood up and loudly stated his simple solution.

"We don't need certificates. All we have to do is have the hides signed by the president of the Real Estate Bank."

The other representatives were baffled by Major Anthony's statement. Many assumed that he was drunk, a not-uncommon occurrence. The only person who really understood what he meant was Colonel Wilson, who also happened to be the president of the Real Estate Bank. He and Major Anthony had long had an adversarial relationship, and he knew that the value of bank notes in circulation with his signature on them was being called into question. Major Anthony, in other words, was saying that a wolf hide with Colonel Wilson's signature on it would be comparable to legal tender issued from his bank. Colonel Wilson's temper flared and he growled at the major.

"Explain yourself, sir!"

Major Anthony remained silent.

The identity of the spirit at the former Arkansas legislature remains a mystery.

"If you will not speak," Colonel Wilson thundered, "then sit down and surrender the floor!"

The major remained on his feet, casually opened up his coat and put his hands on his hips. On his belt, for all to see, was a scabbard with a 12-inch Bowie knife in it. It was apparent to everyone that he was silently challenging Colonel Wilson.

Red with rage, the colonel undid his coat and proved that he too had a Bowie knife. The two men stared at each other as the tension in the room quickly became unbearable. One foolish representative tried to break it by laughing. Thinking that the laughter was a deliberate mockery of himself, the colonel unsheathed his knife and ran towards the major, who in turn drew his knife and tried to meet the colonel halfway.

Grandison Royston, another representative, attempted to separate them by throwing a chair between them. Both men grabbed it and began to thrust at each other with their long knives. Major Anthony managed to slash Colonel Wilson's wrist. Blood began to spurt out, and the adrenaline that surged through him allowed Colonel Wilson to let go of the chair and crouch down under it. The major was so surprised by this move that he offered no defense when the colonel popped up on his side of the chair. With all his might, the colonel thrust the entire length of his knife into the major's chest. The blade reached his heart and killed him where he stood.

The fight took less than half a minute, yet by the end of it Colonel Wilson's ambitions were forever ruined. Although he avoided execution when a jury decided that he committed an excusable homicide, he was kicked out of the assembly. Since he never again held political office, many believe that his is the spirit whose gloom is still felt in the old building. A man who dreamed great things for himself, he saw those dreams vanish in a single act of unthinking rage —reason enough to return after death.

Yet even graver than Colonel Wilson's needless crime was the one attempted by Joseph Brooks. Brooks was so angered by losing the gubernatorial race to Elisha Baxter (and so contemptuous of his proposed reforms) that he tried to take over the office by force.

The 1872 race between Baxter and Brooks, both Republicans, proved to be as dirty as politics could get. Dead men voted. Living men voted more than once, filling out ballots like they were lottery tickets. Ballots were burnt, and voters were threatened at gunpoint at various stations; they were ordered to vote for the gunholder's candidate or suffer the consequences. In the end, because he had more voting territories, Baxter emerged the winner. Brooks was infuriated, since he had rigged the same territories in a previous position. Upon losing, he filed a complaint against his opponent and set about to rectify his loss.

During the two years that followed, Baxter seemed to put corruption behind him and became an honest governor who made good on his promises. The most important of these was his passing a bill that re-enfranchised all the men who lost the vote for their support of the Confederacy. Brooks, who saw this as the end of Republican domination of the state, decided to take action.

Supported by his Republican peers, Brooks staged a revolt. Brooks' complaint from two years before was unearthed, and a Republican judge ruled that Baxter could not hold office. All of a sudden Brooks became the legal governor. Sworn in on the spot, he gathered his men and a large militia and broke into Baxter's office. When Baxter refused to surrender his position right then and there, he was dragged out of his office and thrown out of the building. A cannon was placed at the steps of the building to ensure that he would not return.

He didn't. Instead, he set up his own office a few blocks away. Although Brooks had the support of most of the judiciary and a large army, Baxter refused to give up and formed his own army. Over the month that followed, 200 men died in the small battles that erupted between the two factions. In the end, President Ulysses S. Grant interceded and Baxter was restored as governor.

Brooks survived his coup and even avoided going to jail for it. Surprisingly, he also managed to stay in politics, serving as Arkansas' Postmaster General until his death. But he never forgave himself for his failure to claim the position he coveted most. Consequently, many believe it is he, and not Colonel Wilson, who haunts the old State Building. After all, he remains the only man in the state's history who tried to seize the governorship by force. Such passion could easily lead him to the site of his greatest failure after death.

Often when people wax nostalgic about the past, they describe it as a time of civility and decorum, with the inherent subtext that times certainly have changed. Yet the history of Arkansas' assembly places this attitude in question. While politicians today are certainly guilty of a great variety of indiscretions, it is difficult to imagine them dueling publicly on an assembly floor or using an army to force an opponent out of office. With this in mind, perhaps the identity of the ghost that haunts Arkansas' old State Building is unimportant. What matters is that the people of Arkansas interpret the ghost's despair as a sign that the conduct of the two men should never be repeated.

THE END